The Trouble With Love

Christina Jones

Happy Devi's!

For C.

Christina Jones ♡

This is a work of fiction. Names, characters, places, and scenarios are a direct product of the author's ridiculous imagination. Any resemblance to an actual person, living or dead, any events, locations, or business establishments is entirely coincidental.

Cover art by Christina Jones at Visual Luxe

Chapter One
— & —
Jai
Thursday, April 17th

    Jai kept her eyes focused on the seam of her jeans, running her fingers over the miniscule bumps created by every stitch. She was trying not to think about the angry words that had been exchanged, the look of rage in his eyes, or the sharp impact of his open palm against her face. Obviously, she was failing.

    A look of horror had crossed his face immediately after, and he'd stared down at his hand as if it were part of someone else's body. Jai had slumped to the floor, a confusing bubble of anger, shock, and fear building in her chest. He'd really done it. Elliot actually had the nerve to *hit* her.

    Jai supposed that in a roundabout way, he had a right to be angry. She had been canceling their plans a lot, missing phone calls, ignoring texts. That kind of treatment from someone you had been dating for close to three years had to be grating. Jai knew that it probably hurt.

    What she couldn't understand, was why *he* couldn't seem to understand what was at stake for her. After all, he'd put up half of the money for the 2,500 square foot restaurant. One would think that the investment was an endorsement of her dreams, but apparently not. The time Jai was able to devote to him, to them was diminished from the moment she decided that the restaurant, Honeybee, was going to happen.

    But that didn't excuse *this*. No matter how inattentive she'd been, the mottled bruise that was spreading across her cheek was decidedly not ok.

    Jai toyed with the idea of using makeup to conceal the mark against her skin before Cameron arrived, but decided against it. What would have been the point? Who would she be hiding it from? Certainly not her sister, who was the only person Jai could count on for judgment-free support. Even though Cameron had warned her of the 'vibe' she got from Elliott, the nagging feeling that his 'slight' temper would eventually escalate to more, Jai knew that there would never be an 'I told you so'.

She heard the distinct slam of a car door, and peeked out of the window to see Cameron making her way up to the building, seeming to glide along the walkway in her heels. Jai bit back the surge of jealousy she felt as she thought about Cameron's fiancé, Kyle. He was a *dream*. Physically, he brought to mind Boris Kodjoe, without the pretentious, too-pretty-for-his-own-good vibe. Kyle was handsome, and of course he knew it, but it was an afterthought to him. Never afraid to get his hands dirty, he had spent plenty of his spare time helping get the restaurant open. Hell, he helped more than Elliot did.

Kyle could strike up a conversation with anybody and make friends. He was kind, caring, charming, and smart. All of that was good, but it was the way he treated Cameron that fertilized and watered the seed of envy in Jai. One look into his eyes when she was around, anybody could see that he considered Cameron 'the prototype'. Jai didn't want Kyle, but she wanted *that*. The same warm, palpable, almost intoxicating love that was shared between Cameron and Kyle. Obviously, Elliot wasn't going to be the one to provide that for her.

The sound of the doorbell roused her from her thoughts, and she quickly stood to answer it, nearly tripping over her large duffel bag, which held enough clothes and personal effects that she wouldn't have to return for at least a week. Jai steadied herself, and then opened the door, smiling when her sister immediately pulled her into a hug.

"Where is he?" Cameron was still holding her tight, and Jai sighed when she heard the strain in her voice, a telltale sign that she was holding back tears.

Jai pulled back, brushing her nearly waist-length locs over her shoulder. "I don't know. After he slapped me, he tried to apologize for a while, and then he left."

"Do you wanna call the police?"

"No."

"Has he called?"

"A few times. I didn't answer. Ignored the texts too."

Cameron blew out a breath, visibly relieved as she finally released Jai from their embrace. "Good. He doesn't deserve the opportunity to try to explain anything. Radio silence is all he should get."

"He's part owner of the restaurant, Cam. I can't exactly ignore him forever." Jai shoved her over-sized sunglasses on her face, then bent to pick up the duffel bag at her feet.

Cameron pursed her lips, then pushed a hand through her hair. "I'll buy him out."

"I'll think about that later. For now, can we just go?"

Cameron cocked an eyebrow, but nodded, stepping back so that Jai could close the door behind her. A disarming sense of finality rushed through her as she turned the key in the lock, and it occurred to her that she wasn't even sad about leaving the apartment she'd shared with Elliot for two years. She wasn't even sad that the relationship was over. Instead, she grieved for three years she had given him, and kicked herself for allowing him to be a part of *her* restaurant.

No, it wouldn't be hard at all to move on from Elliot. If she was honest with herself, she already had. Some time around their first argument about her spending 'too much' time at Honeybee, Jai had mentally tapped out, realizing that her vision of the future was critically different from his. Had he expected someone else to run the restaurant? In his mind, would Jai have just been a pretty face to parade around, instead of putting her skills as an accomplished, classically trained chef to use? Did he *really* think she would just sit back and watch while a staff did all of the work, and in turn, had all of the fun?

As she followed Cameron to the elevator, she realized that was exactly what Elliot thought. And therein lied the problem. After three years together, he hadn't really gotten to know her at all.

Hell, he was probably frustrated too.

Three years of wasted time, for both of them. Elliott probably felt like after giving her his time, attention, and money, the least she could do was not spend 14 hours a day away from home. Well, not *probably*, that was exactly how he felt, and he'd said so, right before he accused her of cheating. That allegation led to one of being too controlling, and *that* led to a complaint that she was a 'frigid bitch'. Jai had recoiled away from him after that statement, and then went straight for his manhood.

"Maybe I would be a little warmer if you didn't flounder around like a teenager losing his virginity. Oh, wait. I'm *sure* teenagers probably have more stamina than you."

That's when he slapped her. Jai shook her head as she stepped off of the elevator behind Cameron, flinching at the scorching heat of the sun. It was such a silly statement to make, mostly because it wasn't true. Despite their otherwise tepid relationship, their sex life had never been lukewarm. She was simply attacking because he had, and he lost enough control that he had gotten physical. Elliot's temper had never taken him that far before, but for Jai, once was enough. She tossed her bag into the trunk of Cameron's car, then climbed into the passenger seat.

It was time for a new adventure.

— & —
Cameron
Friday Morning, May 23rd

Even with her eyes closed, Cameron could see him.

Velvety, low-cut black hair. Buttery-soft bronze skin. Strong jaw line, supple lips, and a bare trace of stubble that he would carefully shave away before he left for the office. More than a year ago; before the extravagant engagement ring and upscale apartment, Cameron had studied his face until she knew every detail, committing it to memory, because he was *hers.*

She opened her eyes, then reached out to caress his cheek, allowing her hand to drift down to his shoulder, over a hint of abs, and then lower. She wrapped her fingers around him, gently, beginning a slow stroking motion that she knew would bring him to life. After a few moments, she turned so that her back was to him, pressing her nude body against his. A contented sigh escaped her lips when he draped his arm over her waist, resting his hand against her navel to pull her even closer.

"Again, future Mrs. Morgan?" He spoke the words into the bare skin of her back. His warm baritone rumbled through her, leaving a pleasant warmth lingering in her chest.

"Yes please, Mr. Morgan," she whispered, subtly thrusting her backside against him to emphasize the request.

He skimmed his fingertips along her thighs, only hesitating to ask her about the time before he turned her onto her back, burying his head between them. Even this was an expression of care. He'd already slept through his alarm, and had only been taking an extra "five minutes" when Cameron woke him up. He was nearly obsessive about punctuality, yet he was willing to risk being late to satisfy her need. When it came to her, selflessness seemed to be second nature. Making her happy was as easy to him as breathing, and as Cameron struggled to find her own breath, she hoped that she could give him even a fraction of the peace and sanity that he brought her daily.

When Cameron collapsed onto the bed, with the sheets twined wildly through her fingers, he climbed up to kiss her, leaving the taste of her own sweetness lingering against her lips.

"I've gotta go, Beautiful."

She cupped his ears, pulling him down for another kiss. "I know baby."

Reluctantly, she released him from her grasp, then turned on her side to watch the firm muscles of Kyle's thighs as he ambled to the bathroom. Cameron didn't move until she heard the shower start, swinging her legs over the side of the bed to stand. She arched her back as she stretched into the warm sunlight pouring through the bamboo blinds, frowning a little when the melodic tone of her cell phone reached her ears.

This early? Really?

She sat down on the edge of the bed, lazily reaching for the chiming device. One eyebrow rose when she saw a fairer-skinned replica of her own face on the screen.

Meet me for lunch sis. - Jai

Her eyes flicked to the time. It was barely 8am, which was pretty on par for Jai. Cameron quickly sent back an affirmative response, and then made her way to join Kyle in the shower. He could be a *little* late.

— & —
Jai
Friday Morning

"You alright over there chef?"

Jai didn't look up, choosing instead to keep her eyes trained on the sloppily plated dish in front of her. There was no way she was sending it out a guest. Still ignoring the question -and the persistent ache in her wrists- she carefully rearranged the French toast into a neat pile, then gave it a generous drizzle of the vanilla bourbon cream sauce the patron had specifically requested. After she added a few slices of thick-cut bacon and some fresh strawberries to the plate, it was perfect. Jai quickly passed it on to a waiter for delivery, then finally gave her attention to Brian.

His eyebrow rose as Jai sauntered over, flashing a smile that she hoped would quell his curiosity about her well-being. Brian crossed his arms over his broad chest before he spoke. "You're not fooling anybody, Jai. What's going on with you? Is it Eliot?"

Jai noticeably stiffened at the mention of him.

"No, Brian. Nobody is thinking about Eliot. I'm just tired."

That was mostly true. Eliot had been the last thing on her mind until Brian mentioned him, and she really was tired. But neither of those was the problem.

Jai raised her hands to shakily remove the hair net from her head, revealing her neat, back length locs. When she was done, she rolled her wrists in a circle, trying to relieve the tightness that was becoming a common occurrence. She stopped when she felt Brian looking at her, his eyes narrowing suspiciously as they traveled from her wrists back up to her face.

"Well, brunch service is over, so you go ahead and get out of here. I've got this," Brian said, dismissing what he'd seen as he clapped his hands onto her shoulders. Jai grinned again, enjoying the warmth that radiated from his hands, even through her layers of clothes. She'd met Brian nearly ten years ago at culinary school, and they had been best friends ever since. They finished school together, worked in various kitchens together, and when she decided to open her own restaurant, he didn't hesitate to go with her, and become her sous chef. Brian was more than capable of handling the kitchen. He and the line chefs would make sure that the lunch service ran smoothly.

"You know what? I think I'm going to take you up on that. My sister is meeting me here for lunch anyway. But, I'll be back in a few hours to help get ready for dinner service."

"Ok baby girl. What do you think you wanna eat?"

"What, do I get the honor of eating from Chef Brian's plate instead of one of the line chefs?"

Brian stepped back to give her a playful bow, before turning back to his prep work. "You know I'll cook for you any time Jai. The question is, when am I gonna get a taste of *you*?" Jai's eyes went wide as she looked up at her handsome best friend. Warm brown skin and perfectly groomed black hair that led into a perfectly groomed goatee. Jai knew from experience that his body was solid and firm.

Damn he's fine.

Jai turned away, heat rushing to her cheeks as she processed what he said.

"I see you over there blushing, girl. Relax. I *meant* a taste of your food." He immediately followed that statement with a wink that contradicted it, giving Jai a playful swat on the butt as she exited the kitchen.

In her office, Jai stripped out of her sunny yellow chef's coat and hung it up on a hook. She walked over to her desk, retrieving a bottle of pain relievers from the drawer. She swallowed two, then checked her reflection in the mirror. Knowing that her sister would worry, she pulled out her makeup bag and used her tinted moisturizer to camouflage the dark circles under her eyes. Pleased with the subtle change, Jai swiped her lips with a tinted lip gloss and then pulled her locs from the bun at the top of her head.

It wasn't until she sat down at her desk that she allowed herself to process her latest interaction with Brian. That subtle flirting of his was driving Jai crazy. Not that she didn't enjoy it. That was the problem. She enjoyed the innocent flirtations of her best friend way more than she should, given the fact that he had a girlfriend.

He said it wasn't even serious, but Jai couldn't help sucking her teeth in annoyance at the thought of Brian's girlfriend. *His sexy lady*, she thought bitterly, recalling the pet name he used for Leslie.

"She's not even *that* sexy," Jai said aloud, flinching as soon as the lie rolled off of her lips. Truthfully, Leslie was beautiful. Tall, slim, deep olive skin, and thick, glossy natural curls. Deep-set eyes, perfect little nose, perfect pouty lips. Just perfect. Perfect, perfect, perfect. And if her looks weren't enough, she was a genuinely sweet person. Jai hated her.

A few minutes later, Jai's cell phone rang, alerting her that her sister was waiting on the patio for her lunch date.

— & —
Cameron
Friday Afternoon

"So you don't understand the meaning of the word *discreet*? Your eager tail is gonna get us caught." Cameron kept her voice low, being careful not to draw any unnecessary attention. She was glad that the gorgeous spring weather allowed them to sit outside of the restaurant as they had lunch. It gave her a good reason to keep her oversized sunglasses plastered to her face, camouflaging her eyes as she people-watched against the backdrop of busy midday traffic.

Jai rolled her eyes, but stopped craning her neck, making it obvious that they were sneaking glances at the handsome trio of men a few tables away. "Whatever Cameron. You were the one talking about '*Girl look over there,*' so I looked!" She shrugged as she pulled her locs over the bare bronze skin of her shoulder.

"I didn't expect you to be *so* conspicuous though! Now the one with braids is looking over here-*coming* over here, Jai. With *braids.* Do you see what you got us into?"

Jai covered her mouth to stifle her laugh. "That's so mean, Cam! He's actually cute."

Cameron lowered her voice, leaning low across the table to speak. "*I'm* mean? This grown ass man is sauntering over here with braids in 2014. *That*, my dear, is mean. It's a damn shame too. His face is good, but those braids...honey, *no.*"

She clamped her mouth closed as he approached the table with his eyes focused directly on Jai. He stopped at the edge and smiled, showcasing a set of...

"I'm sorry, are those... *gold fronts*? I don't understa-" she yelped as Jai kicked her under the table.

"Ooops!" Jai said, giving her pointed stare as she turned toward Mr. GoldFronts with a polite smile.

Cameron's phone rang in her lap, flashing a smiling picture of Kyle on the screen. She grinned as she jumped up from the table with a wink at Jai. When she had found a quiet spot, she slid her finger across the screen to answer the call.

"Kyle," she sang into the speaker, pushing her hand into her short hair.

"Hey baby." Cameron sighed as his warm baritone traveled through the line, leaving a pleasant sensation in her chest. "How is my beautiful fiancé doing today?"

"Didn't I just see you this morning?"

"Nah, that wasn't me."

Cameron had to suppress a giggle. "You need me to remind you?"

"Please do. Give me all the details." Kyle cleared his throat, and Cameron imagined him sitting back in his office chair, loosening his tie.

She laughed, pressing her back into the wall behind her. "Not now babe, I'm at Honeybee with Jai. But as soon as we get done, I could come by afterwards..."

"I can't, beautiful. I have a client meeting in ten minutes."

Cameron pouted for a second before remembering that he couldn't see her expression through the phone. "How about a quick visit after your meeting? Could we do that?"

"Of course."

"Thank you, baby," she purred happily, fighting the urge to clap. "Well, I left Jai with some guy that had the nerve to have gold teeth in his mouth, so I should probably get back to her."

"Gold teeth? In 2014?"

"Exactly. I'll see you later babe."

"I love you."

Cameron smiled. "I love you too."

When she returned to the table, there was no mistaking Jai's quiet annoyance.

"Why did you leave me alone with him," she hissed through clenched teeth as Cameron reclaimed her seat. "I should kick your ass."

Cameron raised a hand to her mouth to stifle her laughter. "What? You said he was cute, so I thought you might be interested."

"Liar."

"I'm not! I'm serious; I thought maybe you were *finally* going to try to move on from Elliott, live a little. And if living a little involves a guy who looks like an extra from a '90s rap video, how is that any business of mine?"

It had been nearly a month since Jai's breakup with Elliott, and Cameron was eager for her to get back into dating. She hated knowing that her sister was lonely, and that there was nothing she could do about it.

"I can manage to figure out my own love life just fine," Jai said, breaking into Cameron's drifting thoughts."

"I know that, sis. I just want to see you happy, like Kyle and I."

Jai sat back in her chair and rolled her eyes. "Ohhh, here you go. That must have been him on the phone?"

"Here I go? What is that supposed to be mean?"

"Cam, I've already gotten you together about this once, haven't I? You found your Prince Charming, so you've made it your personal mission to find mine too. *Give it a rest!*"

"I'm sorry, Jai, it's just that-"

"It's just nothing. Talk about something else, *please*. How are things at the magazine?"

Cameron immediately brightened up the mention of Sugar & Spice. "Things are great! I had an idea for something to bring along a little more *spice*."

When she stopped to take a sip from her sweet tea, Jai grew impatient, raising her hands to give a beckoning gesture. "Come on girl, out with it!"

"Well," Cameron smiled, "We're going to do a special feature issue on a bunch of people around the city, and we're going to call it *'Life Savers'*!"

"That can't be it, right? I need more detail than that!"

"Well, I shouldn't be telling you any of this, in case you're some type of spy for the competition, *but I will anyway*! We're going to do men and women, so there are only two real criteria. First, you have to be obviously sexy, no… *interesting* beauty. Second, they have to be in some profession that makes a really big impact on people's lives. Policemen, social workers, doctors, firefighters, hell, we even have some untraditional ones that people don't usually think like teachers, and philanthropists. It's going to be *so* epic!"

Jai had her eyebrow cocked the entire time she was listening to Cameron speak. "And how exactly are you going to get people to agree to this?"

"That was the easy part, actually," Cameron grinned. "We aren't gonna make a profit from the special issue. After we pay the staff, and the printing costs, all proceeds will be split out and donated to a charity of their choice, as long as it's related to their profession. We're also donating all ad revenue from the pages where the feature will be hosted online!"

Impressed, Jai nodded her head. "It's smart. *Really* smart. The magazine looks good for making the donations, and gains a big influx of subscriptions and visitors. The participants get a check and recognition for their charity. It's a win for both sides."

"Exactly! My dream team is out recruiting more people now, even though my photographer has been complaining. He doesn't want to do the sexy shots of the men, but once I threatened to fire him, he straightened up real quick. I would never actually do it, after he's been such an asset these last three years, but he doesn't need to know that. I just need my team to keep it together for me while I'm gone for two weeks on this trip."

Suddenly, the smile dropped from Cameron's face, and she reached over the table to grasp Jai's hand. "I'm gonna miss you when you move out. It's been nice to have you around for this month."

"Oh please," Jai laughed. "You know you and Kyle are ready to have your little love nest back."

"That doesn't mean I'm not gonna miss you!"

"Mmm Hmm. You just make sure you have your ass there tomorrow at 2 to look at this apartment with me."

Cameron scoffed at those words. "*Me?* I'm always on time; you just make sure this restaurant lets you go so that *you* can be there on time. Brian can handle it; it's what you hired him for, right? Not so he could be your little personal eye candy?"

"Right," Jai said, trying to hide the nervous smile that threatened to cross her face at the mention of him.

"Ok then," Cameron nodded, smiling brightly. "I'll see you tomorrow at two."

Chapter Two
— & —
Jai
Saturday, May 24th

Jai rolled her eyes at the message that had just popped up on the screen of her phone. Cameron was supposed to be meeting her so that they could take a second look at a potential apartment. Rather than sticking to the plan, she'd sent a text saying that she and Kyle were taking a 'late lunch', which Jai knew was code for 'laid up somewhere screwing'. She shook her head as she followed the realtor into the apartment. If she had a gorgeous fiancé she'd probably be doing the same thing.

Instead, Jai was dipping into her savings again, for the unexpected cost of finding a new place to live. There was no way she was going back to the apartment with Elliot, and while Cameron and Kyle had been awesome hosts, she was ready to have her own space.

The more time she spent away from him, the more foolish she felt about the length of her relationship with Elliot. The absence only served to highlight their glaring incompatibilities, and Jai cringed when she remembered hoping that he would marry her. That would have been a disaster.

Grateful that they hadn't taken it that far, Jai carefully surveyed what she had already decided would be her new apartment. It was small, but the open-concept loft appealed to her modern sensibilities, and the price appealed to her budget. Best of all, it was in the heart of the city, and a short five-minute walk to Honeybee.

"I'll take it," she said, words that garnered a smile from the realtor, who Jai knew would probably be paid a commission based on the annual rent. The plump redhead gave Jai several pages of paperwork to sign before they left, with a promise that she would be in touch tomorrow about other necessary documents.

Standing alone outside of the apartment that would soon be her new home, Jai felt an unexpected sense of satisfaction. Cameron had bought Elliot's stake in the restaurant, so she was no longer indebted to him for that. Now, with this new place, she could relinquish her part of the lease for the apartment they shared. She ran her fingers over the beautifully engraved '4A' centered on her front door. Somehow, it already felt like home.

"Haven't seen you around here before."

Jai flinched, surprised to hear a masculine voice so close to her. She looked to her side to see a man there, resting on the textured bamboo wallpaper that lined the hall.

She allowed her eyes to trail down to his feet, clad in well-used sneakers, then began a slow sweep back up, traveling over basketball shorts and a sweat dampened tank to reach his face.

"That's because I haven't *been around here* before."

The vivid smile he wore didn't waver in response to Jai's attitude. Instead, it grew wider, as if he could tell that her snippy comeback was an attempt to deflect his attention. He shoved off from the wall and then pushed his hands into his pockets as he took a step closer to Jai. She realized then that her fingers were still caressing new door and snatched her hand away.

"I guess I should welcome you to the neighborhood then."

Despite herself, Jai smiled at the stranger. "What, you live here with your parents or something?"

"Are you serious?" he asked, laughing at her jab against his obvious youth. Even with his neatly groomed mustache and goatee combo, Jai pegged him at no more than maybe 22. Way too young for her to be comparing the warmth of his brown skin to her favorite honey roasted pecans, but she did it anyway.

"Yeah I'm serious. You look like a college kid."

He took another step forward, leaving just a few feet of space between them. "I'm definitely not a kid."

Now that he was closer, Jai could smell him. It was, to Jai, a heavenly blend of the perspiration covering his athletic arms and the Old Spice he'd applied before he did whatever had gotten him so sweaty. She loved that scent, and sometimes even wandered into the men's section at the store just to flip open a bottle and put it up to her nose.

Jai blushed when she realized she'd taken an embarrassingly deep breath to inhale his aroma, then released it as a soft, but audible sigh. When she looked up he was grinning, obviously aware of the effect the close proximity had on her.

"Well," she said, placing her back against the door. "I don't want to hold you up from whatever you were doing."

"Ouch! I can tell when I'm being dismissed, so I'll leave you alone. Can I at least get your name?"

"I don't know you."

He held up a finger, signaling for her to wait as he fished a ring of keys from his pocket. She watched as he strode to the door of the apartment directly across from hers and unlocked it, pushing it far enough for him to flip on the light and allow her to see inside.

"So, now you know where I live, and you know I'm not a college kid. Surely that's enough to tell me your name, neighbor."

Jai tilted her head to the side, weighing her options.

If I tell him now, that's no fun. But if I wait, it gives him a reason to talk me again, which he'll probably think is the intention. And what do I care about fun *with this little boy anyway?*

"It's Jai."

"Pleasure to meet you, Jai. I'm Rashad." He crossed the hall to extend a hand to her, keeping a longer than necessary grip on her fingers. "You look really familiar; do I know you from somewhere?"

Jai held back a laugh. "That's a really cute line, but no, we don't know each other."

"You sure? Maybe college or something?"

"Boy, stop it. You were probably still in elementary school when I graduated."

"Chill with that," Rashad said, chuckling. "I'm 25, thank you very much."

"You say that like its old."

"It's old enough."

Jai cocked an eyebrow, lifting her eyes to meet his. "*Old enough* for what?"

"Grown up things."

His response hung in the air between them for a few seconds before Jai's cheeks grew warm, and she tightened her grip on the purse strap hanging against her shoulder. The gaze he leveled at her made her suddenly feel very exposed, even in the casual jeans and fitted tee-shirt she wore.

"So I'm gonna go ahead and get back to work. I'll see you

around," she said, turning away to hurry down the wide hall. Just before she turned the corner, she stopped fighting the overwhelming desire to look back.

He was still watching.

— & —

Cameron
Friday, June 6th

Cameron's sleek onyx heels clicked against the marble floor as she trekked down the lengthy hall that led to Kyle's office. They hadn't seen each other in several days, because Cameron had been across the country putting out a string of ego-induced fires for Sugar & Spice. After two weeks of stressful meetings and big decisions, she wanted nothing more than to see her fiancé.

The plan was for him to meet her downstairs so that they could have lunch together, but nearly fifteen minutes had passed since the time they'd agreed on. Cameron knew that there were two possibilities. He'd forgotten, which was unlikely, or a meeting with a client had run long. Either way, she was tired of lingering in the stuffy lobby of the building that housed the investment firm he worked for. His own waiting room was much more comfortable.

When she arrived, Cameron noticed that his assistant was missing from his desk, probably gone to lunch himself. She sat down on one of the plush leather couches and pulled out her phone to check Kyle's schedule, which he sent to her every week. Seeing that the last item on his schedule had been nearly two hours before, she pushed herself up and went to his door. She took a moment to check her breath, gave her short raven pixie cut a quick fluff, and then opened the door.

Kyle jumped up from his seat atop the desk when she walked in. "Cameron," he said, a barely detectable strain in his voice. "You're early sweetheart."

"Actually babe, you're late. But I can wait; I didn't realize you were with a client." She smiled apologetically at the woman seated in front of Kyle's desk, taking in her smooth copper complexion and silky chin-length bob. "I'm so sorry Angie, I've barely been back in town an hour, but I just couldn't stay away!"

She'd seen this new client around Kyle's office several times,

19

and had made conversation with her enough times that she knew the woman wasn't bothered that she had imposed. Angie returned her smile as she uncrossed her legs to stand.

"Oh, I can certainly understand that, Cameron. I think we've covered everything we need to for today, so I'm going to go ahead and turn him over to you. I'll see you at our next meeting, Kyle." Angie extended her hand to him, and he shook it, waiting until she left before turning back to Cameron.

He seized her hand, pulling her closer between his open legs until her chest was flush against his, a position that always made Cameron's heart beat a little faster. "I'm so sorry I'm running late, beautiful. That's what I get for relying on that old watch instead of just checking my phone."

She crossed her wrists behind his head, allowing her forearms to rest on his shoulders. "It's fine, Kyle. I wouldn't have barged in like this if I'd known you were with someone. Why wasn't Angie on your schedule?"

"Last minute addition. Do you forgive me?"

"Of course."

He buried his face into the silky dark brown flesh just below her jaw, leaving a trail of feather-light kisses. "Show me."

Cameron smirked, then brought her hands up from the back of his head, running her fingers along his velvety black hair before she cupped his chin. She simply stared at him for a moment, with her bottom lip firmly held between her teeth before she leaned forward, allowing her lips to meet his.

She closed her eyes, basking in the cool sweetness a mint had left on his tongue as he pushed his way into her mouth. His hands fell to her waist, trying in vain to pull her closer as hardness grew between his legs. Cameron broke the kiss, coyly batting her eyes as she nudged him away.

"I think that was more than enough, Mr. Morgan." She brushed imaginary wrinkles from her clothes, shooting him a look of mock disgust as she sauntered away, stopping in front of the floor-to-ceiling window. Kyle pushed himself up from the desk and stalked towards her. The intensity in his lust-darkened hazel eyes made Cameron tremble with anticipation as he approached.

When he reached her, he grabbed her by the thighs, easily lifting her from the floor. "Why are you so damned sexy?" he asked as he placed her down on the desk. She willingly parted her thighs for him when he slid his hand between her knees.

Kyle shifted her dampened panties to the side, thrusting his fingers into her. "Did you miss me last week?" Cameron's legs quivered as he leaned down, capturing her mouth in another kiss.

"You know I did. Did you miss *me*?"

"Without a doubt."

Cameron snaked her hands between them, unbuckling his belt and allowing his pressed slacks to fall to the floor in a heap. She then slid her fingers underneath the waistband of his boxers, pushing them down over his legs.

"Show me."

— & —
Jai
Saturday, June 28th

Jai believed in torture. She had to. That was the only possible explanation for being on Leslie's Facebook page, jealously looking through smiling pictures of her and Brian. She didn't even bother to read the captions, she could do that herself.

Bitch. Bitch. Bitch. Ohh, look at this bitch. Bitch.

Finally, she turned off the screen of the tablet and tossed it across the desk. There was no point in purposely ruining her mood. After two weeks of what had seemed like an endless amount of paperwork, she had finally received the keys to her new apartment, and she could move in. Honeybee had received a rave review in popular local newspaper. Her newly instated work out regimen *finally* had the scale moving in the right direction. All of these were excellent reasons for Jai to be her normally bubbly self.

Instead, she was pissed. Leslie had shown up to have dinner, and being the perfect best friend that she was, Jai had insisted that he leave the kitchen to eat with her. Because having the man she wanted talking and laughing and holding hands with his girlfriend while she sliced, burned, and banged her fingers was a wonderful idea.

Jai could pinpoint the moment that her feelings for Brian had shifted from friendly to romantic. There had been a fight with Elliot. A *bad* one. After she'd screamed herself hoarse dealing with him, she went to Honeybee and called Brian. She had barely finished explaining what happened before he was there, holding her while she cried. Jai felt safe there, pouring out her emotions for him in a way that she refused to do for Eliot.

Three months later, Jai spotted Brian at the movies with Leslie, who he had never mentioned to her. She couldn't quite place the emotion that she felt at the time, but looking back, she knew that the confusing mixture of hurt and blinding anger only meant one thing. She was jealous. Even though she had her own man, she actually envied pretty, perfect Leslie's position on his arm.

This is stupid, Jai thought as she massaged her aching wrists. She should be happy for him. It wasn't like he was the only single man around town. And, even with all of his flirting, he wasn't even interested in her like that.

She looked up at the sound of a knock on the door.

"Come in," she yelled, retrieving her discarded tablet from it's precarious position on the edge of the desk.

"Jai-baby!" Brian sauntered in with a satisfied smile on his face.

Jai averted her eyes, not wanting to think about what Leslie may have done to give him that expression. "What's up B?"

"Did you forget? We're moving you into your new apartment today."

"Yeah, I actually forgot something like that," she said, rolling her eyes.

"Always with the attitude." Brian sat down across from her, supporting his elbows on the sleek black surface of her desk. "Kyle and Cam not coming to help?"

"Nope. You know she just got back home from a trip. She says she wants to spend a quiet night with her boo, so it's just you, me, and the movers on this one. She'll help me unpack this weekend."

Brian rubbed his palms together, giving an exaggerated lick of his lips. "So that means I get to have you to myself later."

Jai only rolled her eyes in response, but the fluttering sensation of butterflies feel her stomach. She wished that he wouldn't do that, making the little innuendo-filled comments. Even though she usually played along, it only confused her feelings for him even more.

"Anyway, are you ready to go? The movers should be there in about 30 minutes and I want to get in before they do." She stood, wiping her sweaty palms over her jeans.

22

"Let's hit it."

Saturday Night

"Let me help you with that."

Before Jai could respond, her new neighbor Rashad was lifting a heavy box from her hands and heading into the building. She wanted to protest, but after she'd dismissed the movers for dropping her box of shot glasses from around the world, she needed competent help. She grabbed a smaller box from the back of the truck and followed Rashad into her first floor apartment.

"Where do you want this to go?" he asked, turning to receive directions.

"You can put it in the kitchen, on the counter." Jai was right behind him, with another box for the kitchen. She placed hers down beside his, and was stepping away to go back to the truck when Rashad grabbed her hand, pulling her close.

"And where do you want *me*?" The corners of his mouth turned up in a bright smile as he stared down at Jai. She bit the inside of her lip, trying not to smile at his persistence.

"It's never gonna happen, neighbor. You may as well give it up."

Rashad clapped a hand over his chest, feigning injury as he dropped his head. "Damn, Jai. Man down, man down."

"You'll heal, young one," she said, lifting her hand to cover his. "I definitely appreciate your help though."

"Why do you keep calling me young? What, you're one of those chicks that only dates older guys?"

"First of all, I don't get the impression that you're campaigning for a *date*. Second, no, I don't *only date older guys*," she teased, mimicking his voice. "But I also don't cradle rob."

"You say that like you're so much older than me."

"Because I *am*."

"Bullshit." He crossed his arms over his chest. "You can't tell me you're older than *maybe* 27. And that's a stretch."

"I'm about to blow your mind then, baby boy. I'm 32."

"Stop lying," Rashad said, waving a dismissive hand. "With that baby face of yours? And I still say I know you from somewhere."

"I promise you don't know me, and I'm not lying."

He closed the short distance between them, boldly allowing his hand to rest at Jai's waist. "I just realized why you look so familiar. I've been seeing you in my dreams," he said, flashing a flirtatious grin. This time, Jai smiled back as she shook her head.

"You're cute, Rashad. Really. But, I can assure you th-"

"What's going on out here?"

Jai and Rashad looked up to see Brian sauntering down the hall from Jai's bedroom. He was shirtless; displaying a lean, honey-toned torso and sculpted abs. Jai stepped away from Rashad's touch, looking frantically between the two men.

"Brian!" She tried not to show how flustered she was by his appearance, but the suddenly high pitch of her voice betrayed her. "This is my neighbor, Rashad. Rashad, this is my friend Brian."

"'Sup, man?" Rashad said, extending a hand in greeting towards Brian, who crossed him arms. Barely suppressing an amused grin from his face, Rashad dropped his hand before turning to Jai. "I'm just gonna go grab a few more of those boxes, ok beautiful?"

"We're good, Bruh." Brian stepped forward, annoyance etched into his handsome features.

"Actually," Jai said, shooting well aimed daggers at Brian, "I would appreciate the help. It's getting late, and the moving company wants their truck back tonight."

"Aye aye, captain," Rashad playfully saluted her before disappearing through the front door.

When Jai turned back to Brian, his expression was still sour. "Ugh. Why are you acting like this B?" she asked, opening the box Rashad had placed on the counter.

"Because I don't like that kid."

"He's not a kid, and you don't even know him."

"I know he had his hands on you."

Jai stopped removing the plates from the box to look up at Brian. "And?"

Brian shrugged. "And I didn't like it."

"So? I don't belong to you."

"Well I may just have to do something about that."

She flung the door of the dishwasher open as her heart slammed in her chest. What did *that* mean?

"Whatever Brian. Did you finish putting together the bed for me?" she asked, suddenly remembering why he'd been in her bedroom.

"I'm done, but don't try to change the subject. Who is he to you?" Brian leaned back against the counter, supporting his weight on his sinewy arms.

Forcing herself to look away from his exposed skin, Jai began loading the unboxed dishes into the machine. "Why do you wanna know, B? What, do you think I'm going to sneak in a secret boyfriend on you, like you did me with Leslie?"

"Leslie was never a secret, I just-"

"Didn't tell your supposed best friend. Right."

"Jai, it wasn't like that."

Their conversation was interrupted by the reappearance of Rashad, carrying several boxes. Grateful for a reason to distance herself from Brian, Jai quickly made her way out of the kitchen. The next several hours were spent in awkward silence, only broken up by Rashad's infectious happiness.

"Thank you, neighbor." Jai smiled at him as he placed the last box down on her living room floor. "You have no idea how much I've appreciated your help."

"I don't know if your 'friend' Brian would say the same. He's been mean-mugging me this whole time."

"He's just being overprotective, don't mind him. Anyway, you should come to my restaurant sometime for dinner. On me, of course, since you helped me move."

"A single dinner? I don't know...I may need a little more than that after all this hard, back-breaking work I did for you today."

Jai cocked an eyebrow at him, catching the coy wink that he gave after his statement. "I appreciated the help, but don't push it, kid."

"Man, you drive a hard bargain," he laughed. "How about you *join* me for that dinner, and we'll call it even."

"Deal."

Rashad gave her a warm, but quick hug before he went to his own apartment, leaving Jai alone with Brian.

"Are you gonna answer my question now?"

Jai groaned. "Damn, you couldn't even let the door completely close before you started, huh?"

"You are avoiding the shit out of this question though, Jai."

"Because I don't get why it matters to you," she said, pulling her locs down from her tight ponytail as she headed down the hall. She stopped in the laundry room for fresh bed linens, and then kept going to her room. She was tired. She wanted to relax under the lavish jet spray of her new shower, then curl up into bed with a book. Arguing with Brian wasn't on her agenda.

In her bedroom, Brian took the sheets from her and tossed them onto the bed before clasping her hands in his. "It matters because *you* matter. I don't want some horny kid sniffing up behind you, harassing you, none of that."

"You sound jealous, B." Jai gently extricated her hands from his, and began making the bed. After a few moments of silence, he helped her.

"What if I am?" he asked, tossing the last pillow against the upholstered headboard before collapsing into the leather recliner that wasn't supposed to be in the room.

"What if you are… what?" She was beginning to get agitated.

"Jealous. What if I'm jealous of another man touching you? What does that mean?"

Jai's eyes shot up from the seam she'd been tracing along the hardwood floor. *Is Brian trying to tell me something?* As she thought back over the last few months, memories of the increased flirtations, sly comments about her being his, and lingering touches came into focus. He'd been complaining more and more about Leslie, and even though Jai had suspected they were just going through usual growing pains, she couldn't help hoping that maybe that was the end. Maybe his smile after dinner had been relief because they were over. Maybe?

Emboldened by that thought, Jai quickly closed the distance between them. She sat down on the plush arm of the chair, turning so that her legs covered his lap. "I'm not sure what that means," she lied. She knew exactly what it meant. He wanted her, just like she wanted him.

He chuckled, patting her against the thigh a few times before he allowed his hand to rest there. "You know I love you, right?"

They had exchanged those words hundreds of times, platonically, over the course of their ten year friendship, but Jai wondered about the timing. Here, now, talking about jealousy… was he trying to send her a message?

Jai shifted, pushing her body closer to him until she could rest her head on his shoulder. "I love you too," she whispered. Their eyes met when he turned his face to look down at her, and before she could second think it, she lifted her lips up to meet his.

"Whoa, Jai!"

She flinched as she hit the floor, a casualty of Brian's sudden decision to leap from the chair. "Ouch!"

"I'm sorry," he said, offering a hand to help her up. "But what are you doing?"

"Kissing you, obviously."

"I know *that*, but why?"

Jai hung her head as tears sprang to her eyes. "Because I thought that there was... I don't know, *something* there. I thought yo-... but obviously not."

She yanked away from his touch when he tried to place a comforting hand against her shoulder.

"Jai... I'm sorry, but I love Leslie. We're serious. *Really* serious."

"Then why are you here, B?" she asked, not-very-gently shoving tears away from eyes with the backs of her hands. "Why all the innuendo, the flirting, the *jealousy*. Huh?"

Brian shrugged himself back into his shirt, covering his bare torso. "We're friends, Jai, why wouldn't I be here to help you move? And the flirting and stuff, that's just what we do. It's what we've always done."

"No, it's been different and you know it." Jai punctuated each word with an angry, embarrassed jab of her pointed finger.

"It has," he admitted. "And that's my bad. Maybe I took things too far, but I never knew that you thought I was being serious. I didn't even think you were into me like that. We're *friends.*"

"Yeah, I see." She shook her head, giving up on the attempt to stop the hot tears flowing down her cheeks.

"Jai, I-"

"It's fine, Brian. You should go home to your girlfriend."

"Come on, do-"

"*Please*." Jai barely recognized the sound of her own voice as she choked back a sob. "Just... go. I'll be fine."

Brian nodded, then did as she requested. He left, making sure to close the door behind him.

— & —

Cameron
Late Saturday Night

Cameron tossed down the bridal magazine and checked her phone for what felt like the hundredth time before lifting her wine glass to her lips. Still no messages, no call, nothing. It was well after midnight, and she hadn't spoken to Kyle since earlier in the day, and he wasn't returning her calls. He had *promised* her that even though he was so busy that he needed to work on a Saturday, he would come home. But, as Cameron's gaze swept over the beautiful meal she'd ordered and set up on the terrace, she finally concluded that he wasn't, in fact, coming home. Kyle never broke his promises. Something was wrong.

She downed her nearly full glass of wine and grabbed her keys, stuffing her feet into the simple ballet flats she kept at the front door.

— & —

Kyle

"We can't do this again."

Kyle looked up from his desk as Angie re-entered his office, pulling the door closed behind her. His heart lurched in his chest as she sauntered toward the desk, smoothing her skirt over her legs after her trip to the bathroom to clean herself up.

"I know… Cameron doesn't deserve this. Hell, neither do you. If things had been different…

Angie sat down on the desktop. "But they weren't. Things happened the way the way they happened. It doesn't make this ok."

"You think I don't know that?" Kyle asked, standing up. He walked around to the front of the desk, stopping in front of her. "You think I don't feel like a piece of shit right now?"

"Kyle." Angie placed a hand soothingly against his chest. "I know you do. That's exactly why we shouldn't let this go any further. We had tonight. Let's leave it at that. Maybe even try to forget it."

He pulled her hand away from his chest, bringing it up to his mouth to kiss. "Angie. I love Cameron, but I will *never* forget you. We—"

"I know," she interrupted, a sad smile on her face. "We shared something special. But again… you're *engaged*. We leave this where it is, and we make sure that she never finds out."

28

Kyle nodded, then placed a kiss against her forehead, allowing it to linger before he moved lower, capturing her lips in a kiss.

— & —

Cameron

In her car, Cameron talked herself out of calling Jai. *She's probably passed out right now,* she thought, suddenly feeling guilty that she hadn't been able to help her sister move into her apartment. If she had known Kyle was going to be so disgustingly late, she could have been there. She *would* have been there, despite her own fatigue from her trip.

By the time she pulled into the parking garage, right beside his car, her agitation had multiplied, and she was ready to flip. Throughout their relationship, Kyle had been a stickler for communication and punctuality. Yet here *he* was, still at work, when he was supposed to spending some much needed quality time. She'd been gone for two weeks! One would think that he missed her, wanted to hear about wedding plan progress, wanted to make up for two weeks of missed sex, but no. His ass wanted to *work.*

She stomped past the barely awake security guard without a word, and punched in the code that would allow her to access the elevator. A few moments later, she stepped onto his floor and headed for his office, pushing through the door.

What she saw took her breath away.

One of Kyle's hands was buried in Angie's hair, the other gripping her waist as he kissed her with a level of passion that Cameron had been sure was reserved for her. *Only her. His fiancé.* She wanted to step forward, say something, anything, but she was rooted to the ground, unable to move or speak. Angie was enjoying it just as much as he was, based on her little whimpers and groans of pleasure. Neither of them noticed that they weren't alone until finally, the door closed behind Cameron with a quiet click that seemed as loud as a gunshot.

They looked up at the same time, breaking away from each as they recognized her. Cameron realized then that she had been released from the spell too, but her brain was rolling so fast that she couldn't even formulate a coherent thought. Kyle reacted first, reaching for her hand as he closed the distance between them.

"Cameron…, baby. Listen, I—"

29

She recoiled, shooting him a look of disgust. "Don't touch me! Did you fuck her?"

He looked panicked. "If you let me explai—"

The hard smack of skin against skin resonated through the room and left Cameron's palm stinging as it left his face. "What is there to explain, Kyle?" She shook her head, taking a step back as Angie stepped forward.

"Cameron, really, it's not wha—"

"*Shut. Up,*" Cameron spat at Angie, who wisely did as she was told, retreating behind the desk. "I don't want to hear anything from either of you."

She wrenched the engagement ring that she had once been proud to wear from her finger. Just before she stepped out of the door, she hurled the now meaningless piece into Kyle's face. He didn't even try to deflect it; he just stood there, with regret filling his eyes.

"I hope she's worth it."

"Cameron, *please.*"

Kyle's fingers closed around her forearm, but she snatched away again. "Please, what Kyle? Huh? Please what? What can you possibly have to say to me after I walked in on you kissing her?"

"It's not what you think, baby, I promise you—"

Cameron laughed. "You what? You *promise*? I thought the *ring* was a promise. What happened to that?"

He raked a hand over his face, pushing out a shaky breath. "It was mistake, babe. A stupid mistake. I swear to you, I—"

"Just... just stop, Kyle." Cameron willed the tears building in her eyes not to fall. "A mistake? Forgetting that I was waiting for you at home, that was a mistake. This? This is not a mistake. I don't know what it is, but it's not a mistake. You don't get to just write this shit off as a *mistake*. No. "

She held up a hand when he tried to speak again. "Don't come back to the apartment tonight."

Without another word, she stepped onto the elevator. It wasn't until she was safe in the steel confines that she cried. Hot, bitter tears that she couldn't seem to stop. After the elevator released her into the lobby, she stumbled blindly to her car, locking herself in. She just needed a few minutes to get it all out, a moment or two for the feeling that her chest was splitting in half to go away.

But it didn't.

It dulled enough that Cameron felt that she could drive, but it didn't go away. It spread across her arms, up her neck, down into stomach, even to her toes. Even her *toes* hurt.

As Cameron maneuvered her car onto the freeway, she tried to clear the image of Kyle and Angie from her mind, but it was so strong that it was burned into her eyelids. Every time she blinked, there it was again, taunting her as she drove along the nearly empty road.

A cheater.

That was something she never, *ever* thought she would have to worry about with Kyle. She'd never even caught him looking at another woman when they were together. From the time they met, at a mixer for young professionals in the city, he had always been all about her. Operative word *had.*

Cameron shook her head as a fresh wave of tears started. What was she supposed to do now? Her head was pounding, and she already felt like she couldn't breathe. Her left hand felt conspicuously empty, almost weightless in the absence of her ring. For a moment, she regretted that she had taken it off.

Had she reacted too quickly? Maybe she should have let him explain. Removing that ring and tossing it into his face like it meant nothing... that was an act of finality. The *end* for their relationship. But Cameron didn't even know if that was what she really wanted.

Her cell phone rang, but she didn't react. She knew it was Kyle, calling to beg her to change her mind. Of course, he would want to explain. Explain what? They hadn't even exchanged vows yet, and he was already being unfaithful.

Ugh!

Cameron bit her lip in frustration as she stopped at a traffic light. When the light finally turned green again, she waited a few beats, then accelerated her car. A second later the thunderous, screeching impact of metal on metal reached her ears. A half second after that, the force of the airbag pinned her to the back of the seat.

Then... there was nothing.

A dull, tingling sort of nothing, accompanied by the metallic taste of blood as it filled her nose and mouth. The traffic on the highway was a muted rumble in her ears, even though she could *almost* feel the vibration as each car passed by. A scream rose to her throat as her body ignored the instructions from her brain to move, get help, do *something*. The sound never came, and Cameron realized with horror that she couldn't even vocalize the confusion coursing through her.

What the hell happened?

Her eyes opened, and she immediately tried to shut them again, to block out the sight of shattered glass still hanging in place of what used to be her windshield. Her brain and body still couldn't seem to make a connection, so they remained frozen open in horror, taking in the now shapeless mess of aluminum that was the hood of her car.

Cool darkness covered Cameron as her eyes finally closed, then opened again on her command. She quickly decided that closed was the better of her two options. Maybe even a nap would be good.

Yes, a nap sounds good.

She tuned out a dull hum, and the faint sounds of a voice in her ear, allowing her suddenly heavy head to fall back against the headrest. Yes, it was definitely time for a nap.

"Ma'am? Ma'am, I need you to talk to me ok?"

What? Leave me alone, I'm trying to sleep.

"Ma'am, these firefighters are going to help get you out of the car, ok? I know you're scared, but I need you to open your eyes and talk to me, ok?"

Didn't you hear me say leave me alone?

Cameron's vision was blurry when she opened her eyes again, trying to find the source of the annoying high-pitched hum. Instead of the clear view she'd had just a moment before, she was inside of a live-action Monet. She blinked, hard, hoping to shift her eyes out of soft focus.

"Can you tell me your name, ma'am?"

Cameron.

"Ma'am, I see that your eyes are open. If you can hear me, can you tell me your name?"

Damn, are you deaf? It's Cameron.

"The firefighters are almost done, and then my partner and I are going to get you in the ambulance and to the hospital."

What?

"Ok, here we go. She's losing a lot of blood, we've gotta get her out of here. Miss, I need you to stay with me, ok?"

Wait a minute, what's going on?

She couldn't feel anyone touching her, but from the shift in view Cameron knew that she was being lifted, and then placed on a stretcher. Nausea swept over her as brightly colored lights flashed around her, seemingly pixilated against the night sky as she was placed into the back of the transport vehicle. She was relieved when the doors closed, blocking the lights and sounds to envelope her in stark whiteness of the inside of the ambulance.

"Ma'am, open your eyes and tell me your name." The same voice from before, but more urgent now, demanding information she'd already given. "I need you to stay with me, and tell me your name."

I already told you my name.

"Ma'am we're on the way to the hospital now, but it would really help if we could tell them your name.

God damn, what's with the name obsession?

"Cameron." She winced as her voice scraped past the dryness in her throat. She barely recognized the croak as her own.

"Ok, Cameron. Do you have a last name?"

"Taylor." The word was barely off of her lips when the tingling feeling in her limbs intensified to discomfort. A second later, it was sharp pain, emanating from Cameron's legs and back. The moment after that, it was agony. Her body involuntarily strained against the straps keeping her safely bound to the stretcher, and she felt a reassuring hand against her arm as the paramedic spoke.

"Sam, where are we on pain relief? She's coming out of shock, and it's gonna be bad."

What?

"Waiting on the ER doc to clear it." That was a woman's voice. The other paramedic?

"Shit. Cameron? Cameron, I need you to try to take some deep breaths for me, ok?"

What? How the hell am I supposed to ta-

The woman spoke again. "Ok, we're cleared. Get her sleeve up."

What?

Cameron felt a sharp poke in her arm, and moments later, there was darkness.

Chapter Three
— & —
Cameron
Tuesday, July 1st

Kyle's quiet snores filtered through the cloud of sluggishness that was holding Cameron's eyelids half closed. Somehow, he had folded his six foot frame onto the tiny pull-out sofa across the room. She forced her eyes to fully open, grimacing in response to the sharp pains radiating from what seemed like her whole body.

Ouuuch.

Her legs were elevated, in splints and thick bandages that stretched from her feet to her knees.

That looks bad.

Ignoring the IV, Cameron pulled the blankets away from her, anxious to see what other damage had been done, but a jolt of pain from her back took her breath away, forcing her back against the pillows.

Breathe, Cameron. Just breathe, just breathe, just breathe.

It wasn't working. The sharp twinge intensified until she couldn't stand it, and began fumbling along the side of the bed for a call button. She needed another shot of whatever they had given her in the ambulance.

"Cameron?"

Kyle's snores had stopped, and he was suddenly beside the bed, his face a mask of concern as he gazed down at her. He looked as helpless as Cameron felt.

"Do you need the nurse? Are you in pain?" he asked, not waiting for an answer before he located and pressed the button that would connect him to the nurse's station. She closed her eyes as she listened to him summon assistance, and didn't open them again until whatever wonder-drug they filtered into her IV began to take effect.

Kyle was still standing there quietly beside the bed, his thick black eyebrows drawn together as he clenched the bedrail.

"What happened?" His face immediately relaxed when Cameron spoke, and he reached forward to grasp her hand. His smooth almond skin contrasted against her chestnut brown, now marred with dozens of cuts and bruises from the accident.

"You were in a really bad accident, Cam. Do you not remember?"

"I know there was an accident, but I don't know what happened."

He shook his head, giving her a humorless smile before he spoke. "Some teenager, drunk *and* texting plowed into your driver's side. He knocked you into the car on your other side, and then you spun into the concrete wall. You're lucky to be alive, babe." He cupped her face in his hand, and for the first time, Cameron noticed that his eyes were shining with tears.

"Don't call me babe. I haven't forgotten. And you can save the tearful act, too." She angled her head away from his touch.

Kyle visibly deflated in response to Cameron's words. "I'm not acting. You're my fiancé; do you really think I have to *act* to be glad that you're alive?"

"*Former* fiancé," she corrected. "Where is Jai? Or my doctor? Or a nurse? I need to talk to someone, anybody but you. Can you relay that to someone on your way out?"

He swept a hand over his face, which was lined with exhaustion. "Cameron, at some point we're going to have to talk."

"You think *this* is that point? I'm in the hospital!" She lay back against the pillows and closed her eyes, feeling the mattress sink down as he sat down beside her on the bed.

"I'm sorry. It's just... it's not what you think, and I want to explain."

"Not interested."

"So you're gonna just give up on us like that?"

Cameron's eyes shot open, fighting against the effects of the painkiller. "*Me*? It's my fault that you decided to screw one of your clients? All those late nights over the last few months, was it her?"

"She's not just a client, sh—"

"Wow. *Wow*. Just-fucking-*wow*, Kyle. Not just a client? So what, you're in love with her too?"

Kyle shoved his hands into his pockets, looking down at the

scuffed surface of his casual boat shoes. "Not exactly. It's more complicated than that."

"It's a yes or no question."

"Then the answer is yes, Cam. I love her. I never stopped."

Cameron willed the wave of nausea that rose in her stomach to go back down. "You never stopped? What does that even mean?"

"Angela is my ex wife."

Tears sprang to her eyes as the gravity of his words sank in.

Cameron knew that Kyle had been married before. Ten years ago, at 24, he had married his college sweetheart. In his words, it was amazing. *She* was amazing. When they conceived their first child, two years into the marriage, they couldn't have possibly been happier. Until one day, a late term miscarriage claimed their baby girl.

Even though they loved each other, they couldn't recover from their loss, and barely six months later, they made the decision to end their marriage. When Cameron met him, three years after his divorce, he still had trouble talking about it. He wasn't lying. He *hadn't* ever stopped loving her.

Before Cameron could decide on a response, a knock came at the door, and a man walked in, pushing a wheelchair.

"Ms. Taylor, I'm Derek Parker, your physical therapist." He reached forward to shake her hand, and before he could speak again, Kyle had shoved his own hand forward, introducing himself as Cameron's fiancé.

"*Former* fiancé," Cameron corrected.

Derek raised an eyebrow, but returned Kyle's gesture before he turned back to Cameron. "I'm gonna be helping to get you walking again."

"Wait a minute; I have to learn to *walk* again?"

Her heart dropped as the smile faded from Derek's face. "Has no one talked about your prognosis with you? You've been here for…," he paused to check her chart, "three days."

"*Three days?*" Cameron turned to Kyle for confirmation. When he gave a quick nod of his head, dizziness flooded her and she closed her eyes. "There's no way I've been out for three days."

"You weren't asleep the whole time. You've been awake a couple of times, just really loopy from the pain meds, anesthesia from the surgeries, all of that," Kyle said.

Cameron's eyes shot open. "Surgeries?"

"Your legs, Ms. Taylor." Derek softened his voice into a soothing timbre that vibrated in her chest as he spoke. "They were shattered. The surgical team put steel rods in your legs, so your bones will heal nicely. That's why you're in splints instead of casts. You have a little bit of a neck and back strain from the impact of the accident, which won't take that long to heal," He said encouragingly. "But I'll be honest with you Ms. Taylor; the open fractures that had to be corrected in your tibia and fibula in both legs are another story. It's gonna take a while before you can put any weight or your legs, and at least a year to be pain free. "

"A year?" Kyle asked, scrubbing a hand over his face again. "That's a long time."

Derek chimed in before Cameron could agree. "Trust me, it'll fly by. I'm going to show you some exercises you can start doing today to keep your muscles strong, and work out a schedule with you for home visits until your doctor clears you to come in to our rehab facility."

"I... I don't know how to process this. This is too much." Cameron shook her head, closing her watery, aching eyes as tightly as she could. "I... can I go home? I just wanna go home, and get back to my life. This... this isn't happening. This *can't* be happeni— get your hands off of me!" She didn't realize she had been shouting until she'd smacked away the hand Kyle had placed on her thigh, intending to comfort her. She didn't want his comfort, she wanted him to leave.

"This is your fault," she said between tearful sobs. "If you had just *come home*, I wouldn't be here. If you hadn't broken your promise this wouldn't be happening, Kyle."

Derek lifted an eyebrow, looking extremely uncomfortable. "... Uh, Ms. Taylor, I'm gonna just come back later to talk to you about scheduling your appointme-"

"No. I'm ready now," Cameron interrupted, taking deep breaths to calm her cries. "Where is my sister? Where's Jai?" she asked, directing the question to Kyle.

"She had to check in on the restaurant. She'll be back soon."

"Okay. I want you to go, and I don't want to see you again." She turned away, focusing on a flower in the wallpaper so she wouldn't have to see the hurt expression on Kyle's face. Why the hell was she feeling bad for him?

"...okay."

Cameron didn't move until she heard the door close behind him.

"Hey… you alright?" Derek stepped closer, placing a hand on the bed rail. She looked up, noticing his startling grey-blue eyes for the first time. That little glimpse of color in the otherwise dreary hospital room did nothing to make her feel any better.

"No," she replied. "But I will be."

— & —
Jai
Thursday, August 21st

"I think we should cut the cheesecake from the menu."

There had never been a time in her life when she wanted to choke someone more than when those words came out of Brian's mouth. That last argument with Elliot was a close second. And Kyle… well, she *did* choke him when she found out that his infidelity had led to Cameron's accident, so that didn't count.

Taking a deep breath, she turned on her heels to face Brian, speaking through clenched teeth. "Everybody loves that cheesecake, it's a crowd favorite. Not to mention, it's my specialty. It stays."

"Yeah, it gets ordered, but it doesn't fit with our young, hip, modern menu." He held up the leather-clad list for emphasis.

"It's dessert. Comfort food. It doesn't have need to 'fit in'."

"That's not your call to make, Jai. I'm the restaurant manager, not you." Brian crossed his arms over his chest, in what Jai interpreted as an attempt to intimidate her. But she wasn't backing down.

"Brian, who hired you?" she asked, crossing her own arms over her chest and cocking an eyebrow.

"You did."

"Okay. Whose name is on the business account that funds your paycheck?"

A muscle twitched in his jaw as he tightened it, mumbling his answer. "Yours, I guess."

"That would be correct." Jai gave him a bright smile as she stepped forward, closing most of the distance between them. "Now just one last question… *Who. Owns. This. Restaurant*? Hmm? Let me give you a hint… It damn sure isn't you. So the next time you decide to open your mouth to tell me something around here isn't my call?

Please remember that your ass is replaceable. My cheesecake stays on the menu, 'kay?"

Jai turned to walk away. She couldn't believe that he actually had the nerve to imply that something wasn't her decision. They were *all* her decisions. Honeybee was her baby, which she had built into a thriving business in just two short years. Most restaurants failed within the first six months of business, where Jai had gone from red to black in that time. And this man thought he was running things? She didn't think so.

"Jai, how long are you gonna hold this shit against me?"

That stopped her in her tracks. His rejection of her had hurt, there was no denying that. But, she could handle that. She could deal. It was what he did after that... *that* was much harder to handle. To her dismay, just the memory drew tears of intense hurt to her eyes.

"I'm not holding anything against you Brian," she said truthfully, not turning around. "I just don't want to take the cheesecake off of the menu. That has nothing to do with you."

Feeling the warmth of his hand on her forearm, she blinked profusely, trying to keep the tears at bay.

"Fine, the cheesecake isn't the relevant part. But your attitude? You've been freezing me out for almost two months, and I don't understand why."

Jai finally turned to him, brushing his hand away from her arm in anger. "You don't understand why? Are you... kidding?"

"I'm not. You won't even talk to me, when would I have had the opportunity?"

"Why don't I just explain it for you then, shall I?" She clasped her hands together in front of her as she spoke. "Two months ago, I kissed you. I did that because obviously I liked you as more than a friend, and you had given me the impression that the same was true for you."

"I tol-"

"Shut up and let me finish," Jai said, holding up a hand for silence. "Now, maybe our friendship could have recovered from that. Who the hell knows? But what we won't recover from- well, I guess I should say what *I* won't recover from is the fact that *a few damn days* after that, you made the decision to propose to Leslie in the middle of my restaurant."

"Really Jai? That's what this is about? You thought I was

trying to throw it in your face or something?"

"Weren't you?"

"No," he said, tossing the menu he'd been holding down onto the counter. "Why would I? I proposed to Leslie here because she loves it here. I had been planning it for months!"

"What?" The tears that had been threatening to drop finally broke free. "We've been friends for a fucking decade, and you didn't mention that you were even *thinking* about proposing to her, Brian. If I had gotten even a hint that you were *there* with her, do you think I would have kissed you? Wow." Jai flexed her aching fingers, then folded her arms over her stomach.

Brian stepped closer, reaching out to wipe the tears from her cheeks. "Jai… any time I mention Leslie, you change the subject. You won't hang out with us. It was obvious that you weren't really feeling her, so why would I come to you to talk about proposing to somebody you don't even like?"

"My only problem with Leslie is that she has what I wanted. She seems like a sweet girl, and I wish you the best, but that's not even the real problem. Why did you propose to her here? In front of me?" Jai knew she was whining, and she hated it. She hated that this entire situation had her emotionally weak, and ready to cry over every little thing.

Grabbing her hands, Brian pulled Jai into a hug. Despite a few verbal protests she accepted the embrace, relaxing into his arms. "I told you," he said, gently stroking her back, "I was just trying to make Leslie happy."

"But at *my* expense. You love her. Ok, I get that. But after that night I kissed you, did it not occur to you at all that maybe you should propose somewhere else? My sister, my *heart*, hadn't even woken up yet. You knew about the accident. You knew I was a mess. I only stopped by the restaurant to check on things before I went back to the hospital to be with Cameron. You could have waited until I left. How do you think it felt for me? I'm already heartbroken, then scared for my sister's life, and you just had to bring me along while you hammered that final nail in the coffin." Jai pushed her way out of Brian's arms, suddenly anxious to be away from him, and he tossed his hands up in defeat.

"I'm sorry, Jai. I really am. I didn't even think about any of that."

Jai gave him a wry smile. "I know you didn't Brian. That's the problem."

She hurried out of the kitchen without giving him time to respond before she tossed her chef's coat into her office and left.

— &—

Thursday Afternoon

Jai went straight for the elevator in Cameron's building, bypassing the door for the stairs. The thought of climbing all the way up to the 7th floor apartment made her knees ache even more than they already did. The heavy metal doors were sliding closed as she approached, and rather than wait, she called out to whoever was inside.

"Hold the elevator, please!"

Jai let out a little sigh of relief when the doors reversed, opening to let her in. "Thank you so much, I really didn't want to wa—"

She stopped speaking, opting instead to just *stare* at the elevator's occupant.

"Are you getting on?" he asked, his lips curling into a smile.

"Huh?" Jai blinked, realizing that instead of getting into the elevator, she was still standing in the foyer. It began to chime, and Jai stepped in just as the doors began to close on their own. "Sorry for holding you up," she said, clutching the strap of the cross-body bag she wore over her fitted tee shirt. *Damn, you're acting like you've never been around a fine man before. And weren't you just crying over Brian?*

"Not a problem. What floor do you need?" Jai's eyes fell to his fingers, which hovered in front of the panel covered with glowing numbers. Seven was already lit.

"Eight." The lie had crossed her lips before she could even think about it very hard, but she didn't correct it. What if they were going the same way? What if he was Cameron's next door neighbor? That would be awkward.

He pressed the button, then gave her a nod before he turned to face the elevator doors. Jai took the opportunity to openly watch him, taking in his muscular back, covered by a bright white polo that contrasted against that smooth golden-brown skin that first caught her attention. Khakis covered long legs, leading down to clean, scuffed

42

boat shoes. She averted her eyes when he glanced behind him, making sure he had room before stepping back to let on another passenger at the 4th floor.

They were beside each other then, and Jai kept her eyes aimed firmly at the ground until the elevator reached the 7th floor. The other passenger exited first, and Jai looked up to see that the handsome stranger had his eyes on her. Gorgeous, steel blue eyes.

Have mercy.

"You have a good afternoon, Beautiful," he said as he stepped out.

Jai's heart thumped out a staccato beat as she raised her hand to offer him a small wave. "You too."

She felt a little sad when he was out of her view, but quickly brushed it off as she left the elevator on the third floor. There was serious thinking to be done before she even entertained the idea of a man again, after the disastrous *three* years she'd given to Elliot. Not to mention the mess she'd now made with Brian.

As she opened the door to the stairwell to get back down to the correct floor, Jai thought about how quickly Elliot's attitude had shifted when he realized she wanted to do more than just *own* Honeybee. For her, having her name on the deed didn't mean anything if she wasn't pumping out the fabulous dishes that kept the restaurant packed for brunch, lunch, and dinner.

Elliot knew plenty about success, but he'd never had to really work for it. Success and money were ingrained in him, and increased exponentially through the generations. By the time Elliot was old enough to take the reins, their family business was lucrative enough that he *really* didn't have to lift a finger. So he didn't.

That wasn't obvious to Jai when they first met, even though Brian had been quick to try to 'warn' her about it. He was charming, dynamic, and *fine*; three of the five qualities that Jai always checked off in her head when considering a new suitor. At 29, she had been feeling the pressure of needing a husband and kids, and the ticking of her "biological clock" was getting louder and louder in her ears. Once she was confident that Elliot was disease-free and not abusive (the other two qualities from her top five), it was easy to ignore the fact that when it came to *real* work, Elliot was lazy. He couldn't understand the satisfaction of accomplishing something with your own hands, instead of just paying someone to do it for you.

Jai shook away thoughts of Elliot *and* Brian as she poked her head out to peek at the seventh floor. The guy from the elevator was nowhere in sight. Relieved, she stepped into the hall and headed for her sister's door, knocking to announce her presence.

"Just a minute!" Jai grinned as she heard her Cameron call through the door. She became a little concerned when several minutes passed without the door opening, so she knocked again. "Damn, I'm coming!" Her voice sounded much closer this time.

A few seconds later, the door swung open to reveal Cameron, standing with the aid of a walker instead of the wheelchair Jai had expected.

"Hey Jai." Cameron said casually, stretching one arm toward her sister for a hug.

Jai stepped forward, closing the distance between them to gently pull her sister into an embrace. "Hey sis! I see you're finally back on your feet, that's awesome!"

"Yeah." Cameron placed her hands back on the walker for support. "My doctor cleared me this morning, and my *wonderful* physical therapist didn't waste any time putting me to work." She cut her eyes behind her to the man who was now making his way into the foyer. Jai simply shook her head. Cameron was always complaining that she hated the guy, but Jai knew it had less to do with who *he* was, and much more to do with the shift in Cameron's demeanor since the accident. "He made me walk all the way over here and answer the door instead of just helping me."

"Cameron, you know I told you last week that I wasn't gonna take it easy on you." Jai's eyes shot up to the therapist's face at the sound of his familiar voice.

Heat rushed to her cheeks as she realized that he was speaking to Cameron, but *looking* at her. It was the guy from the elevator! *Damn*, she thought, remembering the lie she'd told about what floor she was going to. So much for avoiding an awkward moment.

"And I told *you* that you didn't have permission to call me Cameron. It's Ms. Taylor to you." Cameron scowled at the therapist, who responded with a dazzling smile, the same one he'd given Jai in the elevator.

"Don't be like that. Are you gonna introduce me to your... did I hear you say sister?"

"I'm not introducing you to her, not with that hungry ass look

44

on your face," Cam said, cocking an eyebrow at him.

"Don't be rude," Jai scolded as she stepped forward, extending a hand toward him. "Yes, Cameron and I are sisters. Twins, actually. I'm Jaleesa, but everybody calls me Jai."

Her throat went dry as he accepted her hand, but instead of shaking it, lifted it to his mouth to place a kiss there. Her fingers tingled where his lips touched her, send a rush of warmth up her whole arm. "*Very* nice to meet you Jai. I'm Derek Parker." Jai couldn't tear her gaze away from his face, taking in velvety, sandy brown facial hair; lips that she knew were pillow-soft, and again, those striking blue-grey eyes.

"Ok, enough of this," Cameron said, breaking the spell between them. "Sorry to interrupt this little eye-fucking session, but my legs are killing me, can I sit down now?"

"Oh my goodness, I'm sorry Cam!" Jai snatched her hand away and turned to her sister. Derek responded as well, quickly wheeling over Cameron's chair so that she could sit down.

"You did really great today," he said as he pushed her back into her living room. "I actually think the walk to the door was good for your first day. We'll do your stretches, and then if you're feeling up to it we can do some calf raises too, ok?"

Cameron rolled her eyes. "Oh, so you're gonna be nice to me in front of my sister, huh?"

"You think I'm being nice? Let's add some step ups and squats too then." He laughed when Cameron flipped him off. After she moved herself onto the couch, he leaned over to spread a towel at Cameron's feet, then placed a pile of marbles in front of her.

"You know what to do," he said.

Cameron groaned, but dutifully began picking up the marbles with her toes, transferring them to a new pile, and then moving them all back.

"I'm gonna head back to the restaurant, Cam," Jai said, not wanting to interrupt her sister's session. It had been just over 8 weeks since the car accident that had crushed Cam's legs, forcing her into surgery and physical therapy to regain her ability to walk.

"No, wait a minute." Jai was surprised Derek reached out to grab her hand again, sending another round of heat shooting through her fingers. "You said you and Cam are twins?"

"Yes, we are," Cam said as she dropped another marble onto

the pile. "You can't look at us and see that?"

The sisters exchanged a grin as Derek looked back and forth between them. "Same face, different skin tones," Jai said, sitting down beside Cam on the couch. "We're fraternal, but still ended up looking mostly alike."

Jai and Cam shared the same oval face, high cheekbones, and large, expressive eyes framed by thick lashes. They even had similar bodies; tall with long legs, even though Jai liked to keep about twenty more pounds on her than Cameron. There were only two real differences between them. One was their skin; Jai was a bronze, while Cameron dark copper. The other was their hair; Jai had long locs, while Cam kept her hair cropped into a short pixie cut.

"That's interesting. I heard you mention a restaurant?" Derek smirked, but kept his eyes on Jai as Cameron mumbled under her breath that he was nosy.

"Yeah, I own a little place called Honeybee, and I'm also the head chef."

His eyebrows lifted. "Really? That's one of my favorite spots."

"For real?" Jai bit down on her bottom lip to prevent a silly grin from spreading across her face.

"Yeah," he said. "Never had a bad experience."

"What's your favorite dish?" Jai challenged, wondering if he'd actually been there or was just flirting.

"Well, let's see...you make this grilled cheese on ciabatta, with gruyere, bacon, tomatoes, and jalapenos that I think I would *actually* fight somebody over. The chicken and waffle skewers were pretty damn good too. That stuffed pork loin, with the roasted sweet potatoes and asparagus, it was amazing. And that carrot cake cheesecake? Listen, do you have a man? Cause…"

Jai laughed, blushing as she looked down at her hands to avoid his gaze. He had named off several of her favorite dishes. Dishes that were *her* specialties, including the cheesecake that Brian had been trying to take off of the menu. She knew if she looked up, her eyes would betray *exactly* how pleased she was that he was so familiar with her food.

Derek knelt to gather up the marbles from Cameron and put them back in the bag. "Did I pass your test? I've been to Honeybee at least twenty times since it opened last year, but I had no idea the owner was so beautiful."

"I tend to stay behind the scenes," Jai said as heat rushed to her cheeks.

What the hell is happening?!

"But thank you for the compliments on my food. You should stop by the kitchen next time you come in."

"I'm gonna take you up on that."

Their eyes locked for a moment before Jai tore hers away and turned her attention to Cameron, who was watching them with an amused grin.

"Cam, I'll call you later. I should probably get back so I can help Brian with dinner prep."

"Ok baby sis."

Jai rolled her eyes. "You're like, 50 seconds older than me; can you cut it out with the baby sis stuff?"

"We'll be 33 next year, Jai. I've been teasing you about it all this time, do you *really* think I'm gonna stop now?"

"Good point."

Jai said her goodbyes to Cameron and Derek and left, almost reluctant to close the door behind her. She was startled by the pleasant buzz she felt in her chest after meeting Derek, and she was actually excited by the prospect of seeing him again. Maybe they would go on a few dates. After that, she could cook for him. Not like at the restaurant, *just* for him. And then a few more dates. Maybe she would feel those plush lips on places other than just her fingers.

Whoa there. Where is that *coming from?*

Jai blushed as she stepped onto the elevator. Derek was way too sexy, way too smooth if she was already thinking about that kind of thing. She had no desire to end up heartbroken and embarrassed by yet another guy. Between Elliot and Brian, her record wasn't looking very good. By the time she walked out of Cameron's building, she had succeeded in pushing the thought of Derek away from her mind. The only thing she was concerned about was avoiding Brian as much as she could, and making sure she double-checked Honeybee's inventory before the night was over.

I could easily slip under this water… and just stay there.
Cameron's eyes flickered open, focusing again on the
decorative strip of mosaic tile lining the jetted tub. That little detail
was what she'd been focusing on when she fell asleep. Derek would
have as much of a fit as his laid-back demeanor would allow if he
knew she had maneuvered herself into the tub with no assistance, but
Cameron wasn't concerned about that. She was just glad she had the
upper body strength to pull herself from her wheelchair, onto the lip of
the tub, and then down into the soothingly hot water.

She was desperate for relief, in all forms. Emotionally,
mentally, and most of all, physically, she needed an outlet. Relaxing
in the bath seemed like a good idea at the time, but now that the water
had become tepid against her skin, a glass or five of wine was
sounding like the better plan.

Cameron pressed the button to drain the tub, then began the
slow process of dragging herself back to the wheelchair. She didn't
even bother with clothes, opting instead to crank up the heat, and wrap
her shivering body into a thick cotton robe. In the kitchen, she
grabbed the bottle of painkillers from the counter and dumped two into
her hand. Groaning, she realized she would have to go all the way into
the living room for the walker if she wanted a glass from the cabinet.
Spotting the wine refrigerator, which was easily reached from its
position in her lower cabinets, she picked out a bottle, quickly
uncorking it before she changed her mind. She swallowed the pills,
then chased them with a large gulp of the wine.

Cameron kept the wine with her as she wheeled herself back to
the bedroom she had once shared with Kyle. She wasn't surprised
when her phone started ringing. He called every night at this time,
even though whether or not Cameron would answer was always a
gamble. Tonight, she didn't. She sat the wine bottle on the
nightstand, flung the linens back, and pulled herself into the bed.

Sitting up, Cameron reached for the sheets to pull them over
her legs. She flinched when the diamond on her left ring finger flashed
in the low light of her bedside lamp. Closing her eyes, she buried her

hands in the sheets, hiding them from view.

She knew why she had accepted the ring again. She *loved* Kyle. And she knew, despite his infidelity, that he loved her too. So what was so wrong about forgiving him, and moving forward with the wedding? He wouldn't do it again. They would just go back to normal, get married, and live happily as husband and wife. Right?

Cameron rubbed her eyes, dragging her fingers down her face before she reached for the bottle of wine again, taking a long drink. Who was she kidding? Kyle loved Angela too. And why shouldn't he? Under further interrogation, he revealed that at one time, he considered Angela the love of his life. *The one*. How the hell was Cameron supposed to compete with that?

The thing was, Cameron believed him when he said there had only been one time. She also believed him when he said that Angela's intentions for seeking him out had been pure. A relative had died, leaving her an inheritance, so she needed a financial advisor she could trust not to scam her out of the money. So she went to Kyle.

Of course the feelings came rushing back. They had spent nearly 7 years of their lives together. They didn't fall out of love, a tragedy ripped them apart. They had created, then lost, an entire life through no fault of their own. But they didn't lose their love.

When he and Cameron first met, he told her the story of the divorce, but he insisted that he was ready to move on. Three years had passed, it was time. Cameron never saw or felt anything that contradicted that. And for three years, things were perfect. He was perfect. *They* were perfect.

Until one night he forgot to come home.

Cameron took yet another swig from the bottle, disappointed in how light it had become. She had been trying not to blame him for the accident, but the fact remained that if he had simply picked up the phone to say he would be late, or hell, *not* been sharing body parts with his ex wife, it wouldn't have happened. She would have been safe at home, retaining full use of her legs.

But that's not what happened. And here she was, drunk, high on narcotic painkillers, handicapped, and wearing a cheater's ring.

"How fucking stupid can you be?" Cameron asked herself out loud. She poured the last of the wine down her throat, then tucked the empty bottle behind her bed with the rest of the stash that she would dispose of at the end of the week. Feeling her eyelids getting heavier by the second, she turned off the lamp, lowering herself from her seated position. When she finally closed her eyes, a thought occurred to her with a jolt.

She'd never really had Kyle at all. Angela wasn't the 'other woman'. Cameron was.

— & —

Late Saturday Night / Early Sunday Morning

"Cam... what in the world happened?"

"Kyle, you came!" Cameron grinned up at Kyle from her seat on the floor, too tipsy to be embarrassed that she was naked underneath her wine-soaked robe, surrounded by broken glass. "I had... a little accident. My walker is out of reach, and I'm sort of afraid to move with all the glass on the floor."

Kyle shook his head, seemingly confused by the scene in front of him, but he sprang into action to help. He quickly cleaned the up the floor, then allowed Cameron to loop her arm around his neck as he picked her up, carrying her into the bedroom.

"You mind telling me what happened?"

Cameron flopped back into her pillows, crossing her forearms over her eyes. "I just wanted a glass of wine. I couldn't reach with my walker in the way, so I tried to just use the counter... and I ended up on my ass. Dropped the glass, knocked over the wine, everything," she laughed. "I didn't want to hurt myself any worse, so I called you to come help me. And you came!"

"Why do you sound so surprised? You called me at one in the morning saying that you fell, of course I came!"

"I don't know, I... thought you might be with Angela." Cameron dropped her hands to her lap, picking her fingernails to avoid looking at Kyle.

He sat down on the bed in front of her. She could feel him staring, willing her to bring her eyes up to meet his. "I've told you already that I'm not trying to be with Angela. I wasn't with her. I *haven't* been with her."

"So you say."

"It's the truth, Cameron. I know you probably don't believe that, but it is."

Cameron shrugged, looking back down at her hands. "Tell me what happened."

"Babe..."

50

"I know. I said I didn't want to know the details, but now I do. Tell me."

"Cameron... I... okay. Um, about six months ago, I got a call at the office. It was Angela, she needed some investment help. I agreed, and at first, it was just like with any other client. Then... uh... we started talking about other things. Catching up... reminiscing. One thing just led to another, and here we are."

"How many times?" Cameron asked, leaning back into the pillows again.

"I told you, we only slept together once. I know my credibility is in the negative... millions now, but that's the truth. The night you saw us kissing, that was only time."

Cameron scoffed, letting out a peal of humorless laughter. "One more make out session for the road, huh?" Despite her sudden anger, she softened when she saw Kyle's visible deflation.

"I deserve that," he said, running a hand roughly over his face. "I fucked up, and I have to pay for it. I get that. And I'll do whatever I have to do to make it right."

"I don't know that you *can* make it right."

"I get that too."

"Do you love her?"

Kyle sighed, leaning back onto his elbows before he spoke. "When you agreed to take the ring back, I promised you that I wouldn't lie to you again."

"So the answer is yes?"

He nodded. "... Yes."

Cameron closed her eyes, pulling her top lip between her teeth. "If I had died in the accident... would you be with her?"

Kyle sat up and exited the bed, moving to kneel beside her. He reached up and cupped her Cameron's chin in his hand, forcing her to look at him. "Cameron. If you had died... I would be in a fucking psych ward right now. Angela would be the last thing on my mind. Angela *is* the last thing on my mind. I can't tell you that I don't love her, but our time has passed, Cam. You're my future."

"Yeah... so was she, at one time." Cameron turned her head, moving out of Kyle's grasp. She didn't want to see the tears in his eyes. She didn't want to feel bad for him. She needed to keep believing that he was just another sorry ass man who couldn't keep his dick to himself. "My ass hurts," she said, shifting her thoughts to a less emotional subject.

"Do you still have painkillers for your legs? Is it time for a dose?"

"Past time, but I don't want to take them. They'll put me to sleep."

Kyle glanced over the clock. "Well, it *is* nearly 3am, so maybe that's not such a bad thing."

"I don't want to sleep. I want to talk."

"To me?"

"Yes, you. Come lay down with me."

"I can't Cam. I've gotta get back to my own apartment to get some sleep before work."

"You can sleep here." Cameron grinned at the shocked expression on Kyle's face. "All of your stuff is still here anyway. I haven't found the dexterity to burn it all yet."

Kyle laughed as he took off his shoes, then climbed into the bed beside her, taking care to leave her plenty of space. "So what do you want to talk about?"

"I want to talk about the shard of glass that seems to have embedded itself in my butt cheek. Can you see if you can get it?"

"Any excuse to show your ass, huh?" Kyle lifted a small corner of her robe to look at the place she indicated. "Yeah, you're bleeding a little. I'll get you fixed up."

A few minutes later, Cameron was glass-free, and Kyle was gently placing a bandage over the spot. "You want me to kiss it, make it feel better?"

"Kissing my ass isn't necessary… but you can kiss *me*."

Kyle looked up, meeting Cameron's eyes. "Please don't tease me, Babe."

"I'm not teasing. I want you to kiss me."

"You're a little tipsy."

"I'm slightly buzzed, and that's irrelevant. Kiss me."

"I'm not giving you another reason to hate me," Kyle said, shaking his head. "We've never 'just' kissed, remember? It will lead to more, and then you'll be mad at me, so no."

Cameron sucked her teeth. "Angela must have given you some before you came over here, huh?"

"What? Cameron, the last time I had sex was more than two months ago, the night of—"

52

"My accident. The night of my accident, when you fucked *her*."

Kyle dropped his head in shame as Cameron gently swung her legs over the bed to face him. "You owe me," she said, shoving his shoulder.

"What?"

"*You owe me,*" she repeated. "It's been almost three months for us. I was gone out of town, and then I had the accident. We had the quickie in your office the day I got back, but that was it. You owe me."

"Cameron, do you really think sex is what we need right now? We're not even… we're not *good* right now. I know that's my fault, and I want to fix it, but I don't think this is the way to do it."

She rolled her eyes, annoyed by his protests. "You told me earlier that you would do anything to make it right. This is what I want you to do."

"This isn't—"

His words were cut off when Cameron grabbed the front of his shirt and pulled him forward, pressing her lips against his. She closed her eyes, allowing herself to block out everything except the passion of the kiss as he gave in, then took over, invading her mouth with his tongue. When they finally pulled away, they were breathless, and neither of them was interested in stopping at the kiss.

Cameron let out an audible sigh of relief as he unbelted her robe, pushing the thick cotton fabric over her shoulders. Kyle kissed her from her forehead to her toes before he undressed, then made love to her as if he were afraid he would never see her again. He was careful with her, taking care to not aggravate her injured legs. When they were done, he pulled her into his arms, placing a kiss against her head.

"Kyle?" Cameron lifted her head so that she could meet his eyes.

"Yeah?"

"I changed my mind," she whispered. "I want you to go. I can't lay here with you cuddling and pretending that everything is ok. I thought I was ok, but I'm not."

Cameron watched as Kyle swallowed, sending his Adam's apple bobbing. She knew he was checking his own emotions before he spoke, and for a moment, she considered taking her words back, and allowing him to stay.

"Okay," he said before she could speak again. He used his thumb to brush away the line of tears that had escaped down her cheek. "I want you to be comfortable, so I'll go."

"Thank you."

Kyle didn't say another word before he slipped out of the bed, then back into his clothes. He brought Cameron her painkillers and a glass of water, then placed another kiss against her forehead before he left.

She swallowed the pills, then used her walker to get back to the kitchen for another bottle of wine.

— & —
Jai
Monday, September 1st

"Jai? Jai? Chef, are you ok?"

Jai fought the urge to vomit as she stood up straighter, clutching the edge of the counter for balance. Her fingers were stiff, but she managed to stay upright until the wave passed. She felt as if a hammer had been taken to every single joint on her body, and she couldn't have been happier to see that the large clock over the kitchen door read well past 9pm. The kitchen was closed, and she was finally done for the day. She could get home, crawl into a hot bath, then collapse into bed after swallowing as many aspirin as she safely could.

"Chef Taylor?"

"What?" she snapped at the young waiter, who didn't seem to notice her agitation.

"There's a customer who wants to meet you, he's insisting."

Jai rolled her eyes. She appreciated every single customer that came through Honeybee's doors, but she didn't have the strength to make conversation. She barely had the energy to hold herself up after the busy night. Even with her full staff, including Brian, they had been slammed.

"Not tonight, Jamie. Give him my apologies and a gift certificate."

"That's no way to treat your customers, Beautiful."

Jai forced a smile as she turned to see Derek's handsome face behind her. She was genuinely excited to see him, but the pain and

54

stiffness radiating through her body kept her from returning the hug he gave her with any enthusiasm.

"I'm sorry," he said, his expression downcast at her less-than-warm reception. "I shouldn't have just popped up like this."

Jai frowned. "Derek, no. I'm really glad you came, I'm just not feeling very well right now."

His face immediately shifted to concern as he reached out, placing a hand against her arm. "What's wrong? Are you ok?"

"I'll be fine," she assured him. "It's just this weird thing with my joints swelling up and going all stiff. I was already in pain, but after tonight's shift, I swear I feel like I got hit by a truck or something."

"Have you seen anybody about it?"

Jai cocked an eyebrow. "Do I *need* to?"

"Maybe. I might be able to help. Let me go get something from my car, okay?"

Before she could respond, Derek was dashing through the door. Jai decided she needed to get off of her feet, so she went to her office, giving one of the waiters' instructions to show Derek the way. When he came in, Jai was seated on the edge of her desk, not wanting to endure the painful hassle of exiting the office chair when she left.

"These should do the trick," he said, placing a bottle of pills in her hand. "These are *real* anti-inflammatories, not that over the counter bullshit. They shouldn't make you sleepy or anything, but they'll help with the stiffness and swelling until you see your doctor."

"I still have to see a doctor? I thought you were diagnosing me, Mr. Physical Therapist."

Derek laughed. "I can't formally diagnose you, but I've got a feeling that you probably have tendonitis, based on what you described. Let me see your hands."

Jai obliged, sitting the bottle of pills on the desk before presenting her palms to Derek. He took her hands in his, and began a gentle massage that soon had her fingers feeling nimble again.

"That's amazing," Jai gasped as he moved on to her wrists. She tried not to moan as his firm grip brought along what she considered to be sweet relief.

"Is this helping some?"

"Some?" Jai scoffed. "This is the best I've felt all week. Thank you."

Derek playfully brushed his shoulders off before resuming the massage. "I do what I can. Glad I could help."

"I am too. I wasn't expecting you to come by so soon."

"It's been a whole week since we met. I wanted to come that night, but I didn't want you to think I was stalking you or anything."

"Oh please. I would have been glad to see you," she said truthfully. Jai had thought about Derek often in that week. "Is Cameron treating you ok?"

He shrugged. "Nothing I can't handle. She's doing pretty well with her therapy though."

"That's really good to know. I mean, she gives me updates, but she tells what she wants me to know. She's been... different since the accident. That, plus the *mess* with her fiancé... it's just been tough for her."

"Cameron is a little fireball, she'll be ok. I'll have her back on her feet in no time. Hell, maybe this time she can help you kick her fiancé's ass. She told me you like to fight."

Jai groaned, embarrassed as she remembered how she had jumped on Kyle at the hospital. It had taken two security guards to pry her hands from his neck. She was just glad he hadn't pressed charges.

"I don't play about my sister, man," she laughed.

"Yeah, and neither does Cameron. She grilled me for the entire rest of the session after you left that day, making sure I was 'good enough for her *baby* sister'. She must think I have a chance with you."

"And what do you think?"

He grinned. "I'd say my chances were pretty good."

Jai didn't object when he began unbuttoning her chef's coat, then stepped between her legs to access her shoulders. Jai actually welcomed the solid pressure of his hands as they worked out the knots and tension that had been building there.

She blushed as her nipples grew hard in response to the heat radiating from his body. "I've never had a face to face massage before."

"Well, this is my first time giving one. I'm improvising here, Jai." She nearly melted right off the edge of the desk when he flashed her that smile again. Jai suddenly wished she had at least put on a little eyeliner, or some earrings, and her locs were in desperate need of retouching. Of all the days Derek could have come in, did it have to

56

be one of her 'off' days?

"Jai?" She looked up, noticing that Derek's hands had stopped moving. He had those sexy eyes of his focused on her, and Jai instinctively tilted her head back as his fingers trailed along the bare skin between the thick strap of her tank top and her neck.

"What's up?" She asked, wetting her lips with her tongue.

"You never answered my question the other day about if you had a man."

Jai's heart immediately began to race. "I didn't did I?" she asked coyly.

"No, you didn't, but I can't imagine that somebody hasn't already claimed you.

"Why does it matter to you?" She allowed her eyes to meet his. "Are you trying to do some claiming?"

Derek brought his hand up to the side of her face, cupping her chin. When his lips touched hers, they were just as soft as they'd been against her hand the day they met. She parted her mouth willingly, allowing him to explore, taste, and tease with his tongue as he moved his hands down to her waist. She moaned, feeling a familiar throbbing between her thighs as he pulled her closer.

"You had some of my cheesecake," she said, smiling as they finally separated.

"I did, and it tasted almost as good you." He planted another kiss against her lips just as the door to the office swung open.

Jai rolled her eyes as Brian stepped into her office without knocking on the door, eyeing Derek with suspicion. "Hey," he said, staring pointedly at Derek's hands, which were still touching Jai's bare shoulders. "One of the waiters told me you weren't feeling well, so I was coming to check on you."

"I'm fine, Brian." She didn't even bother hiding the annoyance in her voice. Jai had no doubt that the blabber-mouth waiter had *also* told Brian that there was a man in the office with her.

"You must be the happy customer I heard about," Brian said, extending a hand to Derek, who met it with a shake that was visibly over-aggressive. "I'm the manager, Brian Woods. Nice to meet you."

"Derek Parker. I was just… getting to know the gorgeous owner here a little better."

"I can tell. The two of you were looking pretty, uh, *familiar* with each other when I came in."

Jai chose that moment to interrupt, sliding down from the desk.

"Brian, was there anything else you needed to talk to me about tonight?"

"Yes, actually. We need to go over the last minute details for the magazine shoot catering job in a few weeks."

Jai smiled, shaking her head in amusement. "So... no, there's *not* anything that you need to talk to me about right now then. Good night Brian." She put her chef's coat back on, then slid her hand into Derek's. "Come on, I'll walk you out."

"I'm not gonna have to kick his ass over you or anything, am I?" Derek asked as they crossed the parking lot, exchanging numbers.

"Who, Brian? No, he's just being protective."

Derek nodded, but Jai didn't think he looked convinced. "I'm gonna call you later tonight."

"Are you asking or telling?"

"*Telling.*" Derek placed a last, quick kiss against Jai's forehead before he climbed into his car and drove off with a little salute. Jai laughed, returning his wave before she turned, heading for the sidewalk to make the quick trip home to her apartment. She acted like she hadn't seen Brian watching her from the door.

—-&—
Cameron
Tuesday, August 5th

What the hell do you want, Jai? That's what Cameron thought when she saw her sister's pretty face smiling at her through the peephole. But she swallowed those bitter words and plastered a smile on as she opened the door to greet her twin.

"Derek came by the restaurant last night!" Jai wasn't even inside the apartment before she blurted it out, with such a look of rapture on her face that Cameron felt bad that she wasn't interested. Not right now.

"Ugh, seriously Jai? Derek is just about the last person I want to think about. I had the therapy session from hell today, and it really took everything in me to not wring his fucking neck." Cameron ignored the shocked expression on Jai's face as she made her way into the kitchen, picking up the cup she'd been drinking from before the doorbell's interruption. She loved her sister, but she wasn't in the mood for the playful girl talk she knew Jai wanted.

58

"Damn, Cameron. What's with the attitu—" Jai clamped a hand over her mouth. "Cameron, you smell like a liquor cabinet! What is this?" She snatched the cup from Cameron's reach and lifted it to her nose before she took a small sip. "Oh my God, this is damn near straight vodka!"

"It's the flavored stuff, and there's a splash of sprite in there too," Cameron said, trying to minimize it, even though she was slurring her words. She rolled her eyes when Jai poured the contents of the cup down the sink.

"You're not supposed to be drinking *at all*. Liquor messes with your muscle development, which means you're messing up your physical therapy progress. Not to mention you could kill your crazy ass, mixing alcohol with those painkillers!"

"Maybe that's the point."

Shit. Shit-shit-shit-shit-shit.

The flash of rage in her sister's eyes told Cameron she had said the wrong thing. Jai slowly licked her lips, staring a hole into Cameron as her fists clenched at her sides. "I could— no; I *should* smack the shit out of you, Cameron."

"I didn't mean anything by it, Jai. It was jus—"

"It was just what?!" Jai screamed, smacking her hand against the granite countertop. "You wanna be like momma now, Cam? You're gonna turn into a drunk?"

"She was just trying to cope, Jai. You know that."

"Nope," Jai denied, shaking her head. "I don't know anything about that. All I know is that she drank herself into a grave and killed daddy in the process. Apparently, that's what your ass wants to do too, right? Right?"

Cameron pushed out a deep breath through her mouth before she spoke. "Jai...I... the last three months have been hard. Really damn hard. I'm dealing with it however I can, and I don't need you judging me."

"Judging you?" Jai scoffed, throwing her hands up into the air. "You're grown, just like I am. I don't give a shit about you having a drink, but when you start talking about trying to kill yourself, that's a whole other thing."

"Then just forget I said it."

"Cameron," her voice broke as she choked back a sob. "We lost both of our parents because of an alcohol addiction. I can't 'just forget it', because I can't lose you. When you were in the hospital bed after your accident, I literally felt like I was dying. It was like… a piece of me was slipping away, and I couldn't do anything about it. When you said that shit, 'that's the whole point', or whatever you said… you just brought that feeling rushing back. I knew something was off about you, Cameron, but I know you like to deal with stuff alone. I thought you would come to me if you felt like you were losing control."

"What was I supposed to say? I'm a grown ass woman who can't handle a breakup? Ms. Super Fit, always in the gym is struggling with therapy? Was I supposed to tell you that I have nightmares about the accident, sometimes multiple times a night? Nobody wants to hear that shit, Jai."

"I do!" Jai exclaimed, slapping the counter again with her open palm. "We're best friends, Cameron. *Sisters*! Hell yes, you were supposed to come to me about it. I'll kick Kyle *and* that bitch Angie's ass. I'll come do your therapy sessions with you, for moral support. I will come and sleep in the bed with you, do whatever I can to help the nightmares. I wanted to hear it. If it would have kept you from turning to a fucking bottle, hell yes. You. Should. Have. Told me."

Tears welled in Cameron's eyes until she couldn't fight them back. "Jai? …I'm kind of a mess, huh?"

Jai nodded. "Yeah."

Cameron grabbed Jai's hand as tears streamed down her face. "I don't know what to do," she said, between sobs. "Everything is so far from ok…"

"But it will be," Jai assured her. "You're doing great, Cam. You're walking again. Soon you won't even need any help, and you'll be able to start doing more advanced exercises. We'll see if we can find somebody for you to talk to about the nightmares. You'll be back to yourself in no time."

"That's true… but what about Kyle?"

Jai rolled her eyes. "Kyle… is still on my shit list."

"I know that, I'm asking what you think I should do."

Jai squeezed Cameron's hand. "I can't tell you that, sis. It's a decision you have to make for yourself. I know you love him, and he loves you. And he hasn't been with that Angela chick, so—"

"What?" Cameron interrupted. "How do *you* know?"

60

"Oh. Uh… I kinda hired a private investigator to follow him."

"You did *what*?"

Jai pulled her hand from Cameron's. "You heard me. I hired someone to check him out, so I could see exactly how much ass I needed to kick."

Cameron's heart sank, and she cringed when her engagement ring reflected the brilliant light from the chandelier. She hated that she cared so much, but she had to ask. "So… what did you find out?"

Jai shrugged. "Unfortunately — for me, that is— it looks like he was telling you the truth. I had this guy hack Kyle's cell phone, email, hell, everything. From their correspondences, it happened exactly like Kyle said it did, and he hasn't seen her since, even though she's been blowing up his email and cell. He put her on his blocked list, Cameron. So, take all of that as you will."

Cameron nodded as she wiped the tears from her face.

"I'm sorry for blowing up on you like that," Jai said, drying her own eyes. "I just… I don't want to see you ruin your life over something that you can bounce back from."

"No need to apologize, Jai. I get it."

"…How bad is it Cam? Tell me the truth." Jai reached forward, resting her hand on Cameron's shoulder.

"How bad is what?"

"How often are you drinking?"

"… Every day. Usually before bed. Sometimes after bed."

Jai shook her head. "How long has it been going on?"

"Since about a month after the accident."

"Were you drunk the other night when you screwed Kyle?"

Cameron's eyes grew wide as she turned toward her sister. "How on earth do you know about that?"

"Because I heard you two going at it. You called me that night, telling me you fell. I guess you were drunk, and had called Kyle too. I got stuck in traffic, so it took me a minute to get across town, but when I got there and let myself in, I heard you. *Oh Kyle, yes Kyle, please Kyle, hell yeah, Kyle. Just like that. Don't stop,*" Jai laughed as she mimicked Cameron's voice.

"Shut up!"

"Yeah, that's what I started to tell you. Are you always super vocal like that?"

"Oh my God." Cameron covered her face with her hands,

embarrassed.

"Don't be ashamed, honey. I just turned around and left. It sounded like Kyle was taking good care of you."

Cameron looked up from her hands. "Is it bad that I still love him, Jai?"

Jai tilted her head to side, contemplating the question for a moment before she answered. "I can't really answer that for you, but I can say that I don't think it's good *or* bad, Cameron. I think… it just *is*.

Chapter Five
— & —
Jai
Saturday, October 25th

"Is he always all over you like that?"

Jai sighed. Derek had walked in to see Brian's arm draped low around Jai's waist as he whispered what was quite possibly the filthiest joke she'd ever heard into her ear, just before cupping her backside. She was in the middle of a fit of giggles when she looked up, noticing that Derek was standing in the door to Honeybee's kitchen with a stony expression on his face.

She tried to play it off, by wrapping her arms around Derek's neck to offer him a kiss. In front of Brian, he had been cool, but as soon as they were in the parking lot, in the confines of his car, he had asked about it.

"I wouldn't say always, but we play around sometimes. It's really just harmless flirting. Brian and I have known each other a really long time."

Derek shook his head. "Jai, I don't care how long you've known him; I don't like him touching you like that. It's not cool."

Her body immediately tensed. Was he trying to tell her that she and Brian couldn't be friends? She and Derek had only been seeing for less than two months. She liked him. She *really* liked him. But she didn't like the tone this conversation was taking. Could she scale back the flirting with Brian? Sure. Truthfully, she probably should, but their friendship was finally starting to get back on track after 'The Kiss', and she wasn't about to mess that up.

"Derek, you can't tell me what to do, I'm grown."

"Babe," he said, placing a hand over hers. "I'm not trying to tell you what to do; I'm just saying that for me, your interaction with him is inappropriate. I don't think you would like it very much if you saw me somewhere grabbing another girl's ass, would you?"

Jai shrugged. "I don't know. I mean, we've only been dating for two months, and we've barely even kissed. It's not like we're serious, or like we've made anything official. You can touch whoever's ass you want."

Wait, what? What the hell am I saying?

Derek slowly licked his lips, pulling the bottom one between his teeth afterwards. "Wow. That's how you feel, huh?"

No, it's not!

"Yeah, I guess so," she nodded. "Brian has been my friend for ten years, Derek. You're not going to be able to dictate my relationship with him, especially when you aren't even really my boyfriend."

"Got it." He didn't even look at her when he spoke, keeping his eyes trained on the road. "I guess I thought we were something that we... apparently aren't. Good to know where I stand."

"Derek—"

"I'll see you later, Jai." He pulled into the parking lot of her building, staring pointedly at her door until she gathered her purse and climbed out. He drove off without saying another word.

What the hell did I just do?

— & —
Derek
Saturday Night

What the hell did I just do?

He stepped back, allowing Jessica to lower her trembling legs to the floor.

"You have to go," he said, wiping a layer of sweat from his eyes.

Jessica scowled. "What? Why? I thought we were—"

"You thought wrong!" he snapped. This was bad. It was *so* bad. He didn't even really like Jessica anymore. She had just been... convenient.

Derek was mad when he dropped Jai off. And *maybe* his feelings were a little hurt. *Maybe.* But wouldn't anybody's be? He had been under the mistaken impression that Jai was his girl. No, they had never had an official conversation about it, but they were spending every bit of free time they had together. Late night marathon phone calls, trips to the beach, impromptu lunches. In his eyes, they *were* exclusive. And they hadn't even slept together!

He'd been *so* frustrated, angry and hurt that when Jessica showed up, all smooth, almond colored skin, thick wavy hair, and half of a dress, claiming that she had left something the last time she was there. Derek hadn't even talked. He knew why she had *really* come by. He'd just pulled a condom from wallet, pinned her against the wall by the door and drove into her until every bit of anger was gone, and the only thing left was the hurt.

"Derek. I don't know why you keep acting like you don't still want me, when—"

He dropped his face into his hands. "Will you just go, please?"

"Fine. You want me to come back, same time tomorrow?"

"No."

He kept his head lowered until she left, slamming the door behind her.

That was stupid, man. Really fucking stupid.

He jumped, startled when his phone began ringing in his pocket as he headed into the bathroom to wash Jessica's scent from his body.

Jai!

"Hello?"

"Derek?" She sounded uncertain.

"Yeah."

"Are you busy?"

Derek rubbed the back of his neck. "No. What's up?"

"I'm stupid, and I messed up. I got defensive, because I thought you were trying to tell me I couldn't be friends with Brian, so I tried to downplay us. And that was stupid. I was stupid."

"Stop saying that, Jai. You're not stupid," Derek said. "But I wasn't trying to tell you that had to drop your friend. I just don't want old boy putting his hands on you. That's all."

"I know that, now that I've had a chance to think about it without just... *reacting.* Can you forgive me?"

"Of course."

"Are you sure? You're not gonna hold it against me?"

Derek swallowed, guilt lying heavily on his shoulders. "I'll tell you what... how about we just act like today never happened?"

— & —

Cameron
Monday, December 1st

"Shh. Shh, Cam, you're ok, baby. You're safe. *You're safe.* Come back to me, sweetheart."

Heart racing, Cameron panicked for a moment before the room came into focus. She was being held tightly in Kyle's arms as he rocked back and forth, whispering words of comfort into her ear.

"I'm okay, Kyle...," she mumbled into his chest, lifting her head from the folds of his jacket. This wasn't the first time he'd had to pull her out of a nightmare like this, but Cameron had hoped that the last time would be the *last time.*

He brought his hand to her head, burying his fingers in the soft curls at the nape of her neck. "You sure?" Kyle gave a slight shake of his head before pulling Cameron into an embrace. "I *hate* seeing you like that Cam. Tell me what I can-"

"Kyle." She placed a finger against his lips, quieting him. "You've done enough. I'm ok, I promise. It was just another nightmare about the accident."

"It seems like they're happening more often now though. Are you gonna tell Jai?" No. She absolutely wasn't going to tell her sister. Jai had finally backed off a little, giving her room to breathe without checking her breath for alcohol and searching her cabinets. Cameron knew that if she told her about the increased frequency of the grisly dreams, Jai's first inclination would be to question whether she had been drinking.

She hadn't. Sure, this was the third time she was trying to stop, and she'd only been sober a few days, but the point was, she was trying. Wasn't that good enough?

As much as she craved the sweet, subtle tingle against her tongue, Cameron hadn't even indulged in a glass of wine. To keep her mind off of it, she had begun working from home, throwing every bit of energy that she didn't expend in physical therapy into working on the big shoot for the magazine, which would finally be happening the next day.

Cameron shrugged. "She knows." She glanced down, realizing that she had a fistful of his tie in one hand. "Why are you dressed like this right now?"

Kyle sighed, then grabbed her hand, bringing it to his mouth for a kiss. "I'm on my way in to the office, Cam. I was just coming by to check on you."

Cameron's eyes narrowed as tiny prickles of suspicion covered her bare arms. Kyle swore that he wasn't seeing Angela, or anyone else, but she just couldn't shake the nagging feeling that she couldn't trust him. "So I'm supposed to believe that you're heading to work at this time of night? It's-" she glanced at the clock, "7am." Heat rushed to her cheeks as she looked around, finally noticing the early morning sunlight being filtered in through the windows. "Kyle... I'm sorry, I-"

"You're good. I get it." Kyle gave her a tight-lipped smile, then lifted himself from the bed. "I really do have to go. Are you gonna be ok?"

"Yes," she insisted. "*Actually*, I'm going to be better than ok. I'm going to the magazine office today to do our last preparations for the 'Life Savers' shoot tomorrow!"

"That's great baby…. How are you getting there? Do you need me to come back and give you a ride?"

"Nope! Jai is coming to take me to my therapy session this morning, and I'll call a car to take me to my office from there."

"Sounds like you've got it all worked out," Kyle said, nodding his approval. "You know you can let me know if anything changes, right? "

Cameron maneuvered her legs off of the bed, gently lowering her feet to the ground. "Yes, Kyle. I know." She accepted his hand for balance as she pulled herself up. When she was on her feet she released him, ignoring his skeptical reaction to her standing with her own strength.

"Should you be...?"

"Yes, I should. It's fine. Derek actually encouraged me to not rely on the walker so much now. It hurts for sure, but I'm just happy to be using my legs."

Kyle slid his arms around her waist, pulling her close. Despite her small desire to resist, she had to admit to herself that it felt good to be pressed against his warm body. "I'm so proud of you Cam," he murmured into her short cropped hair. Tilting her chin upwards, he placed a kiss against her forehead, then took a chance and dipped lower, gently brushing her lips with his.

Unable to help herself, Cameron released a low moan of consent before she pressed her mouth more firmly into his. "Thank you for coming to check on me."

"You know I'll do anything for you, sweetheart."

"Except stay faithful."

Damn.

Feeling Kyle's body stiffen, she immediately regretted those words. She didn't even know where they had come from. When she made the decision to forgive him, she had resolved to not make him guilty by constantly bringing up his infidelity. What purpose did it serve? To hurt him? Well, it definitely did that, but the problem was that Cameron never felt any better afterwards.

"Kyle…, I-"

"Hey, I fucked up. You don't have to apologize for being hurt." He looked down at his watch with a groan. "I really do have to get out of here, but I love you, ok?"

Cameron only hesitated for a moment before she responded. "I love you too."

—&—

Monday Afternoon

"You can pout all you want Cameron, it doesn't mean anything to me." Derek crossed his arms over his chest as he looked down at Cameron's slumped form. She was supposed to be doing the new flexibility exercises he'd shown her, but she was full of excuses today, and he was tired of it. "Look, if you aren't willing to put in the work, I can give this time to a client who is. So what do you want to do?"

Oh, so now she's *pissed?* He sighed about Cameron's lack of response as he crouched down beside her. "Ms. Taylor, I-" Derek continued his fussing, but stopped when he saw her face. He was surprised by the unshed tears welling in her eyes as she turned her body away from him.

"Hey," he said, immediately softening his tone. "If you're in pain, you're supposed to let me know. We can modify any of these exercises to make sure you're comfortable."

Cameron shook her head. "It's not that, Derek. I'm… I'm fine. I'm sorry about slacking off. Just show me the stretch again, I can do it."

"So you're sitting here crying in the middle of the hospital gym for no reason? That's what you want me to believe?" He reached forward, placing a hand against her shoulder. "Tell me what's going on."

She threw her head back as she pushed out a deep breath. "Well, the magazine is supposed to be doing this big photo shoot tomorrow. It's really important to me, not just for the magazine, but for the money that's going to those charities. Everything was perfect, and then on the way here, I got a call that two of the participants dropped out, and so now I don't have enough people to round out the full 16 that we decided on." Cameron wrapped her arms around her knees, pulling them up to her chest. "I don't know what I'm gonna do. I really needed this to go well, after everything else that's been going on."

"What makes fewer people so bad? That means that each charity gets more money, right?"

"Well yeah, you would think so. But all of the layouts, set design, page counts, all of these things were designed around 16 participants. If we go down to 14, we have pay for a new designs, pay for the printers to reset their run, all of that. So it could end up that *less* money goes to the charities."

Derek grimaced. "Yikes. None of your people know anyone else that can fill in?"

"Not on short notice. This shoot has uh… very specific criteria."

"Such as…?"

"Well," Cameron said, clasping her hands together. "They have to be in a profession that makes a drastic, positive difference in people's lives and they have to be attractive. Of course there are people who will visit the site, and buy the print copy, and donate just out of the goodness of the hearts. Which is great. But most people are gonna keep coming back to the website, sharing it, and telling their friends because of the sexy pictures of sexy people. *That's* where the real money is gonna come from."

Derek nodded his head. "You're definitely right about that. I wish there was something I could do for you. But, let me show you this stretch agai— "

"Whoa, whoa, whoa. I just thought of something," Cameron said, a smile spreading across her face. "You're a handsome guy, Derek. And not that I was looking, but you've got a nice body underneath that tee sh— "

"Nope, let me stop you right there. I'm not doing it."

"Why not?!"

Derek wiped a hand across his face. "Come on, Cameron, it's just not my kinda thing."

"But you'd be doing me such a big favor. And it's for charity! Think about the people you could help!"

"Yeah, including *you*."

Cameron shrugged. "Yes, including me. Please, Derek. You're a good fit for this. Physically, you're perfect. And come on; look at all of the people you help around here as a physical therapist. I know you have clients that are lot more messed up than me, and you get these people moving again, you give them hope. I'm actually not sure why I didn't ask you before."

"Because you don't even like me! You've been giving me hell about putting in the necessary work since day one. I push you, and I don't back down from your bullshit. You can't stand that," Derek said, shaking his head as he stood, ignoring Cameron's hands as they motioned for him to help her up.

"See, that right there is why you think I don't like you. You won't even help me get up, but if I get mad about it, all of sudden you're the victim!"

"No victims here, Cam. I won't help you do anything you can do yourself. Get up. *On your own.*"

He grinned as he watched Cameron maneuver herself up from the floor, cursing the entire time.

"You happy now, drill sergeant?"

"Hell yeah! As a matter of fact, I am. Aren't you?"

Cameron tilted her head to the side, thinking for a moment before a smile returned to her lips. "Actually... yeah."

"Now you get it? If I was always stepping in for you, taking it easy on you, do you really think you'd be able to do that right now? Six months after your legs got shattered?"

"... I guess not."

"What?" Derek exclaimed, raising his arms to flex his biceps. "Give me my props, come on!"

"Oh, shut up! I *was* complimenting you, and you weren't trying to hear it!"

He lifted his hand to stroke his chin. "Okay, I'm listening now. I'm not doing this photo shoot, but you can tell me more about how perfect I am."

"You know what?" Cameron asked, wagging her finger at him. "Never mind. You're doing too much. I'm gonna just tell Jai that you don't wash your hands, or something equally gross. I bet she makes you keep your grubby little fingers and mouth to yourself after that. Humph."

Derek's eyes widened. "You're gonna blackmail me into doing this shoot with false information?"

"If I have to." Cameron crossed her arms over her chest with a smug grin. "But all I have to do is mention the idea to my sister, and she's gonna make you do it anyway."

"Make me?" Derek sucked his teeth. "Whatever, Cameron. I'm a grown ass man, y'all aren't gonna *make me* do anything."

"Okay. I'll see you at our next session."

Cameron could practically see his mind working as she pulled on her jacket to leave. She waved as the turned around, heading outside.

"Cameron!" He called, jogging up to her just as she opened the front door. She stopped, turning to give him a questioning look.

"What's up?"

"I'll do it."

Derek shook his head as a smile spread across Cameron's face. "*Really*? You'll really do it?!"

"As long as you don't bad mouth me to your sister."

Cameron clapped her hand over her mouth to suppress a laugh. "Derek, I wasn't serious about that! I wouldn't interfere with you guys, it's not my business!"

"That shit wasn't funny, Cam."

"... sorry. But will you still do it? Please?" She grabbed his hands, squeezing them between her own.

"Yes, I'll still do it."

Cameron threw her arms around his neck, pulling him into a hug. "Thank you! I knew you were good for *something*," she laughed as she squeezed him tight. "Hey… I bet you probably have a handsome physical therapist friend or doctor around here don't you?"

"Cameron, I'm not looking at these dudes like that, wh-"

"Oh please, Derek. Every man says that, but you guys scope out competition just like women do. So let me put it to you like this… do you have a friend, co worker, acquaintance, *whatever*, whose job

71

fits the criteria for my shoot, and who you *wouldn't* want around Jai?"

Derek opened his mouth to protest, but was interrupted by his phone buzzing with an incoming call. He smirked at the name that popped up on the screen. "Cameron... it's your lucky day."

— *&*—

Cameron
Monday Evening

Cameron's seven-person staff breathed a collective sigh of relief as she relayed the news that the dropouts had been replaced. When the meeting adjourned, she kept back the three key people that she referred to as her 'dream team'. Cameron had hired them right out of college, so they were young, but very capable. While most people had been unwilling to take a chance on them because they lacked experience, Cameron was a believer in potential. Because of that, she had scored two extremely talented writers and a brilliant photographer, all of whom she was able to groom to fit Sugar & Spice's specific needs.

Glancing to her right, Cameron caught the eye of her photographer. He was slumped back in his seat with a bored expression as he flipped a pen through his fingers.

"What's with the little grumpy vibe you're giving me right now?" Cameron asked as she checked off items from her 'to-do' list. She knew exactly what his problem was, but she was curious about whether he would admit it.

"Cam, you know I don't wanna take a bunch of corny pictures of half-naked, oiled up dudes."

She cocked an eyebrow at him, placing her list down on the table. "So you want me to hire a new photographer then?"

"No," he grumbled.

"Good. Then perk up some. I let you have full creative freedom over the direction of the shoot, and you came up with a great idea. Don't know why you're minimizing it to 'corny oiled dudes'. Besides, you're forgetting the... let me see...*six* gorgeous women that you get to shoot."

He clapped his hands together, with suddenly renewed energy about the project. "*Now* we're talking."

"Uh, slow your roll, Rashad. I *forbid* you to sleep with any of these women, and I am *not* playing. I haven't forgotten that crazy

72

internet guru heifer that hacked my damn website after you did… whatever the hell you did that had her going psycho."

"I already told you Cam, di— "

"Do not sit here and say 'dick too bomb' to me," Cameron interrupted. "Don't you do it. You're 26 years old; it can't be that damn good."

"I'm perfectly willing to give you a test drive if you thi-"

Cameron shot him a murderous look, which Rashad wisely took as a warning to stop talking.

"Anyway," she said, giving him a last look of disgust before she turned to the writers, Audrey and Natalie. "Everything else is a go. The loft space is clean, the sets have been delivered, all participants have confirmed, and I talked to Jai from Honeybee this morning. They'll be there an hour before the shoot to do their catering set up."

"Wait, Honeybee is doing the food for the shoot?" Rashad asked, sitting up in his chair.

Cameron squinted at him in disbelief as she answered. "Uh, yeah. We've been talking about this for months. Do you listen at all in these meetings?"

"Only when it's about the photos." He didn't look the least bit ashamed to admit that as he leaned forward onto the table. "But, hey… is Jai gonna be there?"

"She is… why are concerned about if my sister is gonna be there or not?"

Rashad snapped his fingers with a triumphant smile. "*That's* what it is!"

"What are you talking about?"

"Nothing at all, boss lady. Just realized something that I should have realized a *while* ago. I think my 'eye' is slipping."

Cameron wanted to press the issue, but she knew that getting into a circular argument with Rashad over the disgusting things that went on in his head wasn't a good use of her time. "Uh huh. So, anyway, that's all for today. I will see you guys bright and early tomorrow for this shoot. I need you guys well rested and ready to go!"

— & —
Rashad
Monday Night

Just the person I wanted to see, Rashad thought as he spotted

Jai in the lobby of their building. She looked good, he observed, just like she always did, in riding boots, dark jeans that fit her like a second skin, and a thick white sweater.

"Jai!" he called out, almost hesitantly. He was enjoying his view from behind her, and wasn't in a hurry to have it taken away. She stopped, her locs swinging behind her in a long ponytail as she turned.

"Hey Rashad." She smiled, a sight that always made Rashad's heart pump a little faster. He was used to doing the charming, not the other way around. The thing was, Jai wasn't even trying. After he closed the distance between them, he hugged her, a liberty he took as often as possible since she didn't seem to mind. Today, he kept his hands a respectable distance from her backside, giving her a slight squeeze before he released her from his embrace.

"I haven't seen you in a minute." He took her grocery bags from her as they started down the hall. "You been hiding out or something?"

"No, I've just been crazy busy. Between the restaurant and helping my sister, I really only come here a few hours a day to sleep. Get home late and leave early."

"Yeah, I keep odd hours too; I guess we just keep missing each other. So what are you cooking for us tonight?" he asked, holding up the cloth bags. Getting invited in for dinner was usually the first step to becoming 'that' kind of neighbor, so he figured he may as well get the ball rolling.

Jai laughed. "Us, huh? I wasn't doing anything too fancy, just grilled chicken, pasta, probably a salad. I guess I have enough for two."

Rashad stepped aside to allow her to unlock her door, then followed her into her kitchen, watching her hips as they swayed back and forth. "You sure? I won't be interrupting anything?"

"Yes, I'm sure. I'm actually glad for the company, maybe it will keep me from freaking out."

"Freaking out?" Rashad placed the bags on the counter, and after a nod from Jai, began unpacking them.

"Honeybee has its first catering job tomorrow, and I'm trying not to stress out about it. My sister's magazine is doing a photo shoot, and she asked me to do the food for her."

Rashad averted his eyes as he pulled a package of chicken

breasts out. "Why are you nervous if it's for your sister?"

"Why wouldn't I be?" Jai countered. "It's just as important, maybe even *more* important that I do a good job for her. She was in a really bad car accident, and this is the first big thing she's done since then. I want this to be perfect for her."

"Sounds like you really care about her."

"Well, duh, she's my sister. Besides that, Sugar & Spice is kind of a big deal. It's one of the most popular magazines for black women."

"Oh wow, that's pretty cool." Rashad had to turn away to hide the pride that crept across his face from hearing the praise for Sugar & Spice. It was Cameron's baby, no doubt, but Rashad had put plenty of hours into it as well. When he glanced back, Jai had a huge grin on her face as she filled a pot of water for the pasta.

"Yeah, I'm really proud of her. We hardly ever talk about work when we get together, because we usually just want to think about anything else, but when she *does* talk about it? You can just hear the love in her voice. Even when she's frustrated and stressed, you know?"

Rashad nodded, thinking about the way that Jai's eyes lit up whenever she talked about Honeybee. The restaurant was actually one of the few things he had ever talked about with Jai. They usually only saw each other in passing, so they never had time for much conversation. He was surprised when he found himself missing her over the last month. He knew she had a sister who had been in an accident, but her lack of specifics hadn't given him any hints that she could have been talking about Cameron.

At least he knew why Jai looked so familiar to him now. She had the same face as the woman he had been working for over the last four years.

"Hey," she said, placing a hand against his shoulder. "You think you could chop these veggies for me? I'm gonna go change into something I can cook in, if that's ok?"

Rashad promptly had a vision of her stepping back into the kitchen in heels, and nothing else. "Please do. Take your time."

His fantasy didn't quite pan out, and he couldn't help feeling a little irrationally disappointed about the yoga pants and tank top that covered her curvy body when she returned. She immediately went to work, bustling about the kitchen to prepare their meal.

"So I noticed," Jai said, sitting down beside him at the bar, "Earlier you said that you keep odd hours. You've never told me what it is that you do, Rashad."

He quickly stuffed his last forkful of pasta into his mouth, stalling while he thought of an answer. He could have just told her that he worked with Cameron, but he decided that there wasn't any fun in that. "What do you *think* I do?"

"Hmm." Jai stopped eating, resting her chin on her hands while she looked Rashad over. "I don't know, you're kinda hard to read... I say dope boy." Her eyes glittered with laughter as she raised her glass to her lips, then stood to take her plate to the sink.

"Damn, a dope boy? In these clothes?" He asked, indicating his bright white polo and jeans. "Alright then, I'm not even gonna correct you. Just gonna let you roll with that."

Rashad found himself drawn to her as she rinsed her dishes, so he went along with the urge to walk up behind her, slipping his arms around her waist. He was glad that she'd left her hair in a ponytail, because it gave him the opening he needed to place a kiss against the bare skin of the back of her neck.

"What are you doing, Rashad?" She pulled away, shifting her head to the side so that she could see him.

Rashad breathed in the clean scent of her perfume. "I'm just trying to see something."

"Uh uh," she said, turning to face him. "I told you before there was nothing here for you."

"Oh really?" Rashad lowered his mouth to hers, but was met by her index finger instead. "Rashad... stop."
Shit.

He groaned, but dropped his hands and took a step back to give her some space. "Come on, Jai, what's up?"

"What's up is that I'm not about to sleep with you."

"Just let me put the he-"

"Get out!" Jai shouted with laughter as she playfully slapped Rashad's chest. "You play too much, so you gotta go."

"All the teasing you've been doing about me being too young, but you won't even let me prove myself? What am I supposed to do with this?" He said in a pleading voice, gesturing towards the erection that was quickly making its presence known. Jai's eyes lingered at his crotch, her lips slightly parted before she finally looked away, shaking her head.

"Uh, I'm sure you have some little girl your age on booty call standby, so don't you dare try to make me feel bad. Come on now," she said, grabbing his hand to lead him to the door. "I'll see you around, neighbor."

Rashad grinned as she pushed him into the hall, swiftly closing the door behind him.

Oh, she wanted me. He had a bounce in his step as he walked to his own apartment to make a call. To one of the girls on standby.

Chapter Six
— & —
Cameron
Tuesday, December 2nd

Cameron kept her smile to herself as she watched Rashad direct the model, who was a pediatric surgeon, around the set. It had been an amazing morning, but she couldn't praise her staff quite yet. They were only through most of the participants, but they had a few left to go. There was a lot that could go wrong. For the moment, she was content with quiet satisfaction.

"Cameron!" She took her eyes away from the heavy flirting of the photographer at the sound of Jai's sharp whisper. Her sister looked annoyed, which was out of character for laid-back Jai. Or at least, it used to be.

"What's going on, Jai? Why are you looking so frazzled?"

Jai cast her eyes around the room, making sure that no one was in earshot before she knelt beside her sister to speak.

"The photographer!"

Cameron raised an eyebrow as she gave a slight shake of her head. "You're gonna have to give me more than, hon'. What about him?"

"That's *the* neighbor I was telling you about!"

"Rashad?!" Cameron clamped a hand over her mouth, realizing that she had practically yelled his name for the entire room to hear. She furtively glanced in his direction, hoping that he hadn't heard. No luck. He was grinning right at them, and even had the nerve to wink at Jai before he turned back to his task.

"Ugh, thanks big mouth! Now he knows we were talking about him!" Jai groaned in frustration, laying her head down on Cameron's lap.

"Girl, who cares? It's *Rashad*," Cameron said, her voice tinged with mild disgust. "I mean, I would be lying if I said his little young self wasn't sexy, but he is *such* a whore, Jai. It's almost amazing. Like… I'm sure he's slept with at least 5% of the city's female population."

"I live across the hall from the man, don't you think I see the parade of women he has in and out of there?"

"And yet, if Derek weren't in the picture…"

Jai's head popped up from Cameron's lap. "What are you trying to say, Cam?"

"I'm not trying to say anything. I'm *saying* that you would have screwed him, and your ass would probably be at the gynecologist right now asking for all of the antibiotics you could get. Are you listening to me?" Cameron snapped her fingers in Jai's face, but she didn't react. She was looking past Cameron, in the direction of the empty offices that Sugar & Spice was using as makeshift dressing rooms for the shoot.

"*Damn.*" Cameron's throat went dry at the sight of the two men walking down the hall toward them. She fumbled for her sister's hand, clasping their fingers together when they met. "I need you to pinch me Jai, there's no way he's this fine."

But he was. Cameron's eyes skipped right over Derek to take in the sight of the man beside him. Through sheer willpower, she was able to pull herself somewhat gracefully to her feet, but she still had to tilt her head up to see the deep brown eyes, dimples, and beautifully full lips of the stranger's face. She knew it was cliché, but as her eyes traveled down to the deeply sculpted abs revealed by his open shirt, she couldn't help thinking of the Hershey bars she and Jai would share as kids, greedily licking the melted chocolate from their fingers when they were done. She glanced back at Jai, wondering if she was thinking the same thing, but she was too occupied by the sight of a shirtless Derek to see anything else.

Not trusting herself to not stare, Cameron looked to her hands instead. Her eyes immediately fell on her engagement ring.

Shit.

She was perfectly willing to be a victim in her situation with Kyle, yet here she was practically drooling over some guy she didn't know.

"Cam?" Derek said, breaking her away from her guilty thoughts. "This is my homeboy Will. When I told him about your project, he volunteered. So here we are."

Cameron extended a hand toward Will, quietly gasping at the electric warmth that shot up her arm when he accepted it with a firm shake. She took a little breath, clearing her thoughts before she spoke. "Nice to meet you, Will. Thank you for helping us out today."

"Not a problem at all." He tilted his head to the side, furrowing his brow at her in curiosity until a slow smile spread across his face. "I know you."

Cameron's eyes widened as she looked to Derek for confirmation, but he shrugged, turning back to Jai.

"Will said your name was Cameron, but it didn't connect until I saw you." To her surprise, he put a finger underneath her chin, lifting it to survey her face. "You look a hell of a lot better than you did the last time I saw you."

Moving away from the unexpected touch, she shook her head. "I'm really good at faces, Will, but I don't remember you. I think you have me mixed up with someone else."

"Definitely not. You were pretty out of it."

Cameron furrowed her brow, trying her best to remember how she knew him. "Can I have a hint?"

Will rubbed a hand across the bottom of his chin, pretending to think it over. After a few moments, he leaned down, speaking quietly into her ear. "I pulled you out of what was left of your car after your this summer."

Ma'am, open your eyes and tell me your name.

Cameron stepped back, clamping a hand over her mouth as recognition washed over her. His face, as handsome as it was, held no memories for her, but his voice? For the past 6 months, hearing it in her sleep had been the difference between whether her recurring dream would simply be a recollection of the accident, or a much worse nightmare.

If his warm, soothing tones were present, pleading with her to open her eyes, everything would be ok. But if her ears were met, as they too often were, with deafening, suffocating silence, it was a different experience altogether.

Tears sprang to Cameron's eyes as she puzzled over the appropriate response. Was she supposed to shake his hand again? Give him a hug? She was saved from her confusion by the approach of an intern, carrying a vibrant bouquet of roses.

Momentarily distracted, Cameron pulled the card out of the

flowers, smiling when she realized they were from Kyle.

"Good luck today, Future Mrs. Morgan!" -Kyle

Warmth spread through her chest as she read the message. *This* was the sweet, thoughtful Kyle she knew. She wasn't familiar with the cheater. Feeling eyes on her, she looked up to see that Jai, Derek, and Will all had smirks on their faces as they watched her.

Cameron cocked an eyebrow as her lips turned up at the corners. "What is it?"

"The look on your face," Jai said. "You look like you just got asked to prom by your secret crush."

"Whatever Jai! Now back to you…" Cameron turned her attention to Will. "I don't really know what to say. Thank you seems… inadequate."

"I didn't tell you to get a thank you; I just thought it was cool. I hardly ever see the people I help again. Hell, I honestly thought you were gonna die. You lost a ton of blood; the air bag busted your face up, and your legs… I'm surprised you even still have them. It was like you didn't have bones anymore, it-"

"Will!" Cameron glanced thankfully to Derek, who had noticed how uncomfortable she was hearing the information. Hearing about the accident from Will's perspective had her feeling weak-kneed and sick to her stomach. "Chill with that, man. She doesn't want to hear that right now."

"Shit. I'm sorry. Got a little carried away." Blood began returning to Cameron's face as he apologized with a sheepish grin.

"Ya think?" Jai mumbled under her breath as she placed an arm around her sister's waist. "You ok sis?"

"Yeah, I'm fine. It's just…it's hard to think about still," Cameron explained to Will. "But, like I said, I'm fine. So, let's get to this photo shoot. One of you guys can go next!" She turned, heading to where Rashad was reviewing photos from the screen of his camera.

"What's up boss lady?" He looked up as she approached, allowing his eyes to linger on Jai, who was staring up at Derek with adoration in her eyes. He smirked at the scene before he turned back to Cameron. "One of these guys next?"

"Yes. The one Jai is making googly-eyes at is my physical therapist, Derek. You know Jai, right? Your neighbor? My sister?" She shot him a wilting look, hoping he would catch the admonishment in her words, but he just continued grinning, oblivious. "Anyway, our other model is Will, who is a paramedic. He was actually the one who responded to the scene of my accident."

"Wow. Nice to meet you guys." Rashad stood, shaking both men's hands before he directed his attention to his boss. "Hey, why don't you all do a few shots together, and Audrey or Natalie can do a story for the feature. It would be cool to talk about the personal connection there."

"It's a good idea, but I'm not exactly photo shoot ready right now." Cameron said, mentally picturing the yellow sweater-dress, tights, and simple flats she had put on that morning.

Jai sucked her teeth. "Girl, whatever. That's what wardrobe is for. I'm sure they have something you can put on."

"Jai, shut up. This is supposed to be a *sexy* photo shoot. I'm not putting on any of those skimpy clothes!"

She continued protesting as Jai dragged her over to the racks filled with different wardrobe options. "So... Will is pretty nice looking, huh?"

Cameron rolled her eyes, lifting her left hand to wiggle her ring in Jai's face. "I'm not looking at Will. I'm engaged, remember?"

"Oh yeah," Jai said dismissively as she held up a black cocktail dress with a tulle skirt. "This works. Find some shoes."

"I can't wear flat with this dress."

Jai cut her eyes in Cameron's direction. "So... don't wear flats with this dress. It's not like you're gonna be walking in the heels. Rashad can shoot you sitting down or something." She held up a pair of bright pink peep toe stilettos. "Let's go."

A few minutes later, Cameron was experiencing the most fun she'd had since the accident. Together, Derek, Will, and Rashad had her laughing until her sides hurt, and she felt confident and pretty in the short dress and high heels, even though she had a hard time standing on them. She grimaced as she thought about the hassle of learning to walk in heels again, but it was quickly replaced with a smile. Who gave a damn about walking in stilettos? The fact that she was walking at all, largely thanks to the two men beside her, was as close to a miracle as she'd ever experienced.

Her laughter rang out through the whole room when Will and Derek, both shirtless, lifted her from her feet, draping her across their arms. Spontaneously, she threw her arms up, pointing her toes toward the sky as Rashad engaged the shutter to take their final frame.

This day was going great after all!

Jai
Tuesday Afternoon

Jai was thrilled to see the happiness radiating from her sister. With her flawless copper skin and jet black hair, Cameron was already a striking woman, but the pure joy on her face in that moment took her to an entirely new level.

No wonder Will can't stop staring, she mused, watching as he and Derek gently placed Cameron back on her feet. Physically, Will was closer to Jai's type than Derek was, with his tall, sinewy body and rich mahogany skin. Yet, her eyes always went back to Derek. Sandy-brown hair, golden-brown skin, and a light, even layer of slightly darker freckles. He and his friend were very similar in build, but where Will was all deep, dark browns, Derek was gold.

Except for those damn eyes of his.

Jai blushed when she realized that Derek was staring right at her. He winked before turning back to listen to what Cameron was saying to he and Will.

"Jai!" She looked over her shoulder to see Brian headed her way, a slight frown clouding what used to be a perpetual smile.

"What are you doing here, Brian?"

He looked past her, his scowl deepening when he spotted Derek. "I just came to check on things, make sure it was going smoothly for you. What's he doing here?" He jutted his chin in Derek's direction as he crossed his arms.

"He's one of the shoot participants, Cameron's physical therapist," Jai responded, giving Brian a weary look. Since he had walked in on them in the office at Honeybee, Brian had been peppering her with questions about Derek, all of which she generally refused to answer. He hadn't bothered to be forthcoming with information about Leslie, so she didn't really see why she should divulge the full story between her and Derek.

"So that's how you two met?"

Jai blew out a deep breath as she rolled her eyes. "Yes, Brian. That's how we met. Now, as you can see, everything is fine here. You should get back to the restaurant, isn't it almost time for dinner prep?"

"Yeah. As long as you know what you're doing." He left that cryptic statement in the air as he continued looking past Jai to glower at Derek. Suddenly, his expression turned even darker. "Hey, isn't that the smart-mouthed kid from your building?"

He was pointing directly at Rashad. Jai dropped her head as she pinched the bridge of her nose, wondering how she had found herself mixed up into a confusing love... rhombus? Parallelogram? Whatever it was, Jai wasn't amused. "I don't know about any of that, but my adult neighbor, Rashad is here because he's Cameron's photographer."

"So Cameron is just introducing you to people left and right, huh? That's... cozy."

Jai's nostrils flared as she bit the inside of her lip, trying to remain calm. "Brian, I don't know when you became this bitter, cynical, unpleasant guy, but it's not a good look. You need to stop."

"What are you talking about?"

"You're really gonna act like you don't know that you've been acting like an asshole? Look, I know that I was the one who caused the initial awkwardness between us. After that, I can admit that I was distant, because I was hurt, but you getting in my face about Derek and Rashad isn't cool. I never acted like this about Leslie."

Brian pushed out a sigh as he stuffed his hands into his pockets. "I'm not trying to be a jerk, Jai. I just see these guys sniffing around you, and I don't wanna see you get hurt again, like with Elliott."

"Nobody is 'sniffing around me'. Well... maybe Rashad, but I can handle myself. The attraction that I have with Derek is mutual, and I want to explore that without you looking like someone kicked your puppy every time he's around."

"But, I-"

She placed a hand against his forearm, quieting him. "Brian, we're friends, right? I mean, still?"

"Of course we're still friends, Jai."

"Okay then. As my friend, I need you to back off with the macho shit. Can you do that?"

Jai was relieved to see Brian's glowering expression slowly fade into a smile. "I guess I could do that," he said, pulling her into a hug. As she allowed herself to relax into his embrace, she felt like a weight was lifted from her shoulders. It would take some time for things to be back like they were, before 'the kiss', but she was happy that they were finally moving forward. For a moment, she wondered if Brian would really make the effort to not antagonize Derek, but she quickly brushed away her doubts. If nothing else, Brian had always been a man of his word.

— &—
Kyle
Wednesday, December 17th

Kyle kicked his feet up onto his desk as he massaged his temples. He was trying to relieve the massive headache that had blossomed like a mushroom cloud during the meeting he had just finished. The client was widow at 70 years old, and had somehow convinced herself that Kyle was trying to steal her money. Why she wouldn't just go to someone else he didn't know, but he *did* know that after meeting with her, he was left feeling like it maybe wouldn't be so bad to just jump out of a window.

When the tension in his forehead dissipated, he sat up, pulling up his schedule on the desktop. He was free for at least another hour. Glancing at the time, he wondered if he had enough time to run by Cameron's office for a surprise visit. The pink and white diamond bracelet he'd picked out for her was 'burning a hole in his pocket'. He couldn't wait to see her reaction.

He pressed the button on his desk phone that would connect him directly to his assistant's headset. "Stephen, there aren't any clients out there waiting for me, are there?" The last thing he wanted was to be held up in the waiting room by a talkative client who had nothing better to do than arrive insanely early for appointments. Kyle frowned when he didn't receive an immediate answer. "Stephen, you there?" He glanced at the clock again. It was well past lunch time, and Stephen always made sure to notify Kyle if he was leaving.

"This is odd," Kyle said to himself as he stood, heading for his office door. As he approached, he heard the muffled sound of people arguing. One, he recognized as his assistant. The other was a female voice that didn't register until he opened the door and stepped out. "Angela?"

Angela and Stephen stopped arguing to look towards Kyle.

Stephen was clearly agitated, but Angela's face held a look of triumph.

"What's going on out here?" Kyle asked, directing the question to Stephen.

The assistant glared at Angela before he spoke. "I was telling this... woman... that you were on a tight scheduled, and could not be disturbed. She insisted that she would just wait until you had a moment, and when I asked her to please leave, she got belligerent. I was just about to call up security to come and get her." Kyle nodded to Stephen, pleased that he was following the instructions he had already been given about how to handle a visit from Angela.

"Please, Kyle. I just need a minute of your time to talk to you." Angela stepped forward, directly into Kyle's path. "You won't answer any of my calls, respond to any messages. I've been trying to get in touch with you for the last six months."

Inwardly, Kyle groaned. He had been diligent in making sure he had absolutely no contact with Angela, because he didn't want anything to mess up the possibility of repairing his relationship with Cameron. Even now, he still only felt love for Angela, but he knew their time together was in the past, where he should have left it. Cameron was his future, and that's what he was focused on.

"Angela, I haven't been in contact for a reason. I'm trying to fix things with my fiancé, and I don't think your presence helps that process."

"I know that, Kyle. I'm not trying to get in the way of that. I'm *not* a home wrecker, but we do have something we need to talk about."

Kyle shook his head. "No, we don't. I put you in touch with a great financial advisor; he'll take good care of you."

Angela let out a heavy sigh as she stared up at Kyle. "I'm not talking about tha—"

"Then there's noth—"

"I'm pregnant."

Those two simple words seemed to hit him like a freight train, taking away his annoyance that she wouldn't just leave him alone, and replacing it with an almost overwhelming emotion that he couldn't decipher. He watched as she unbuttoned her heavy wool coat, revealing a rounded belly that looked almost comical against her petite frame. Just like before.

He remembered being in an almost constant state of bliss as he watched his pregnant wife. Decorating the nursery, buying baby clothes, and choosing names had become a part of his reality, replacing drunken nights at strip clubs with his friends. He was different. He had a wife. He had a family. *His* little family. For a while, everything was perfect. Until one morning, it wasn't.

A lump rose in his throat as he fought the urge to touch her stomach.

"Kyle?" His eyes rose to meet Angela's, which were wet with tears. "It's not exactly the type of thing you leave on a voicemail, or send in an email, you know? I know you're with someone, and like I said, I'm not trying to get in the way of that. I... I just wanted to give you the chance to be in his life."

"His?"

Angela nodded, using the sleeve of her coat to wipe her eyes. "Yeah. It's a boy this time. Look, this wasn't planned. When I found out, I considered...not having it, but after losing Kylie, that wasn't happening." She wrapped her arms protectively across her belly. "I understand if you don't want to have anything to do with him, Kyle. You have a new life, and a fiancé, and I don't expect you to rip that up for me. I couldn't just *not* tell you though."

"I want to be in his life," Kyle said, without hesitation. He was confused as hell by his feelings for Angela, but he knew without a doubt that any child of his would know their father. "Besides, Cameron isn't the kind of woman that would be ok with me not acknowledging my child. The entire situation is uh... delicate, but we'll make it work. We have to. I think Cameron will understand."

"You're right."

All three heads turned at the sound of Cameron's voice from the doorway that led to the elevator. Kyle's heart sank at the hurt he saw reflected in her eyes as she slowly approached the group.

"Cameron... baby, liste-"

"Kyle. It's ok." She stared down at Angela's belly before looking back to Kyle. "But... I *can't* do this. Not a baby. If you cheated on me after being around her for a few months, how am I supposed to get comfortable with a permanent reason for her to be present in your life?"

Kyle caught her hands in his as she tried to slip the engagement ring from her finger. "Cameron, *please.* I'm trying so hard to make it right, baby."

"I know you are, and I appreciate that. I do. But…." She shook her head. "This can't be made right Kyle. I won't do this myself. I won't spend the rest of my life wondering if *you're* spending the rest of your life wondering 'what if '. I don't deserve that. I don't deserve to have to hope that you're not making another baby every time you're with her. You're torn, Kyle. It's all over your face. I can't settle for that."

Tears welled in Kyle's eyes as Cameron pulled her hands from his and gently removed the ring. She pushed it into his hand just as her own tears sprang free. Kyle hated the feeling of finality that enveloped him when their fingers no longer touched. He wanted to protest. How could she possibly tell him what he was feeling? He wanted to tell her she was being silly, that there was no way of knowing what the future would hold. But he couldn't, because he knew she was right.

She was shaking when he pulled her into his arms. She openly sobbed against him, a heart-wrenching sound that made him want to kick his own ass. When she finally looked up, her eyes were swollen, and he face soaked with tears.

"I'm so sorry I let you down, Beautiful. I'm sorry for the accident. I'm sorry for hurting you. I'm sorry for *everything.* I love you."

Cameron simply nodded before she pushed her way out of his arms. She paused for just a moment, staring at Angela before she turned back.

"I love you too, Kyle… goodbye."

She was gone before Kyle could even process his response.

— & —
Will
Friday, December 19th

Will wasn't even sure why he let his baby brother drag him into this piece of shit bar. A damn cop bar. Neither of them were even cops! But Wes had a thing for the women in blue, so Will was spending his Friday night surrounded by drunk ass police officers in a raggedy dive bar. While Wes complained. Perfect. A perfect fucking way to start the weekend.

"-and I guess you think you're what, now? A model or some shit?" Wes slurred, sloshing his beer on the table as he pointed the bottle in Will's direction. "And you couldn't even call *me*? I'm the handsome brother, not you. And, I'm a firefighter. When was the last time you ran your ass in a burning building to save somebody's bad ass little kids? *Never*, motherfucker. That's when! 'Life Savers' my ass."

Here we fucking go, Will thought, unamused as his brother rambled off the extensive list of issues he had with Will's participation in the shoot for Sugar & Spice magazine. Wes was still talking –and being ignored– when Ms. Sugar & Spice herself walked through the door.

Will actually did a double-take, surprised to see Cameron looking so… unpolished. It was a marked difference from the perfectly together woman he'd met earlier in the month. It took him a moment to realize that the only real change was in her face. Gone was immensely happy expression she wore when he left. Its replacement was a look of confused dejection as she made her way to a seat at the bar. A *cop* bar. What the hell was she doing in a cop bar?

He could still hear Wes railing on and on about why he hadn't been called about the shoot, but Will's eyes were locked on Cameron as she gulped back a shot of something brown, then requested another. And another. In a cop bar.

Interesting.

By the time she made it to her sixth shot, Wes had attached himself to a pretty Latina police officer. Literally. He was damn near sucking the woman's face off, so Will, unwillingly to play audience to their show, made his way to Cameron. He was still several feet away when he heard her voice, several levels louder than were necessary in the crowded bar. When he realized that she was arguing with the bartender, he began moving a little faster, reaching her just in time to prevent her from snatching the guy by the front of his shirt.

Suddenly, the entire bar was quiet. Will groaned as the eyes of at least a third of the city's police force turned to Cameron, who was now shrieking at the top of her lungs about the bartender's 'fucking audacity' to cut her off. Noticing one *very* sober looking cop in particular as he approached, Will instinctively placed his hand over her mouth, effectively stopping her rant. "*Shut the fuck up before you get your ass arrested in here,*" he mumbled into her ear as he wrapped a protective arm around her waist.

"Are we gonna have a problem here, Will?" The burly man

asked, placing a hand against the taser hooked to his belt.

Will's eyes flicked to the device, then back up to the man, catching his meaning as Cameron struggled against him. "Nope, not all. The lady just had a little too much drink, but I got it. Everything is good—ouch! Shit!"

"I don't even know you!" Cameron finally succeeded in getting Will's hand away from her mouth by biting his fingers, causing him to pull away.

Will glared at her as he clenched his hand, trying to use pressure to take away the pain. "I was just with your crazy ass all day a few weeks ago, on my day off, by the way. Excuse me for trying to help!"

Cameron continued shooting him the same cold, crazed look of anger before recognition warmed her eyes. "Wait a minute…Will? WILL! Heyyy!"

Oh, damn. She's one of those split-personality drunks. Fucking great, Will thought as she threw her arms around him, embracing him like an old friend. The hostile glares of the other bar patrons switched to amused sympathy for Will as he carefully dragged her away from the bar.

"Drunk and disorderly in a bar full of cops, huh?"

Cameron shot him a scathing look as she slid her purse from shoulder and began rummaging in it for something. "I'm… not... drunk," she said, her undeliberately slow speech contradicting her words "I'm just… a little… tipsy is all. But since I'm causing such *prob*-lems, in front of the *po*-lice, I guess I'll just go home." She finally succeeded in digging the keys from her purse, holding them triumphantly in front of her.

"And how exactly do you think you're getting there?" Will picked the keys from her hand, holding them out of her reach. "I know you don't think you're about to drive? I'll call you a cab."

"I'm fine to drive."

"You're drunk as hell; you're not fine to drive."

Cameron snatched for the keys, smacking him in the chest when he lifted them higher that her 5'7" frame could possibly reach. "It's not your business anyway. I said I wasn't drunk, so give me my keys, Will."

"So you can kill yourself or someone else? Hell no."

"Fine, I'll just tell one of these officers that you stole my property from me!"

Will cocked an eyebrow at her, daring her to do any such thing. "Would that be before or after you fail a breathalyzer?"

Her eyes shot daggers straight for his heart, but her lack of verbal response told her his comments had hit home.

"Actually," he continued, "Come on. I'm taking you home myself."

"What? You know, you have a lot of fuc-"

"Yeah, yeah. Blah blah blah." He grabbed her by the hand, pulling her out of the club and into the cold, crisp December air. They could still hear the sounds of the bar crowd; only it was now muffled against the snowy night sky. "How did you end up here anyway?"

"Here?"

"This raggedy-ass cop bar."

"It was the first place I spotted when I decided I needed a drink." Her breathing hitched as she purposely dragged her feet, making it harder for Will to pull her along to his truck. "Not the best choice, since apparently I couldn't just be left alone to mind my business."

Will grinned as he fished his keys from his pocket. "Mind your business? You were a centimeter away from having your hand around the bartender's throat. That ain't 'minding your business', sorry."

Pressing the button on his keys to unlock the door, Will found himself wondering why he even gave a shit, since she obviously didn't. The first reasons hit him as she was helping her into the truck. Derek was his best friend, and he happened to be very interested in Cameron's sister. Will could hear Jai now, fussing at Derek. "*Why are you friends with the kind of asshole that would see my sister in trouble and not help?*" In turn, he would have to hear Derek's mouth about it. As he closed the car door, it also occurred to him that his friend cared about Cameron independently of her sister. He'd spent a lot of time and effort getting her mobile, and from the way Derek spoke about her, he could tell they'd developed a weird sort of *almost* friendship. He could hear Derek now. "*What the fuck kinda dude are you that you couldn't help my friend out?*"

So, as Will saw it, even though helping her was really just the right thing to do, he was doing Derek a favor. That thought was the only thing that preserved his sanity through the forty minute drive — complicated by her nonsensical directions— to get Cameron home, during which she alternated between uncontrollable crying and hurling nearly-incoherent insults his way. By the time he got her to her apartment, he was ready to simply shove her through the door and leave, but seeing her state of agitation he didn't quite feel comfortable leaving her alone.

As she stormed from room to room, Will pulled out his phone and dialed Derek's number. When he didn't receive an answer, he hung up without leaving a voicemail, deciding instead to send his friend a text.

"Yo, I need you to tell Jai I had to rescue a bartender from her drunk ass sister. I got her home, but she's wilding out, and I'm not trying to deal with this shit." -Will

"Will you stop all that damn pacing?" Her seeming inability to stop moving was only making Will's headache worse.

Cameron shot a dirty look over her shoulder as he followed her into the kitchen, where she finally sat down. "You know you don't have to be here, right? I'm an adult, and I'm perfectly capable of taking care of myself."

"Yeah. Right."

"What the hell is that supposed to mean?"

"Did. I. Fucking. Stutter? I don't know a single 'capable' adult who thinks it's a good idea to get drunk and pick a fight in a bar full of cops. I don't know any 'capable' adults that then decide 'ok, I'm drunk, let me get behind the wheel of car! That's a great idea!' You of all people should know better than to take a chance with somebody else's life." There it was. The *other* reason he gave a shit about any of this situation. And suddenly, he was really, really pissed.

"Did you forget that six months ago some dumb ass drunk almost killed you? The surgeries, rehab, none of that shit affected you enough that you would think twice about putting yourself in a situation to do that happened to someone else? You can't be that stupid."

"Excuse you, asshole. You don't know me."

She narrowed her eyes at Will as he stepped closer to her seated position at the counter. "Thank. God," he said, right into her face. "Cause I really can't stomach selfish ass people like you who put others at risk with their shitty decisions. I've had to pull *kids* out of mangled cars because someone just like *you* decided they were 'just a little drunk' and ended up killing whole fucking families. Cause your life is just so bad that you have to drown your little feelings." He

92

didn't even care that he was yelling at her, and she was flinching with every word. She was scared? Good.

Maybe a little fear would keep her ass in line the next time she wanted to drink and drive. Even though Will knew it was irrational, he took it personally that after she'd been able to, after a while at least, walk away from an accident that could have easily ended her life, she was cavalier enough to *willingly* risk it.

"What happened, somebody hurt your feelings?"

Her head shot up, and Will didn't miss the way her right hand flew to cover the left in a protective gesture. "Like I said. You don't know me, so shut up!"

A slow smile crept across Will's face. He had hit a nerve. "Ohh, I see. Your fiancé. What did he do, forget to pick up your fancy rice from Whole Foods or something?" he asked, remembering the huge diamond she wore and the flowers she'd received while he was at the Sugar & Spice offices.

The impact of her hand across his face immediately took away his smile. Cameron was standing now too, staring him down like a bull. "I said shut up! You don't talk about him." The sight of unshed tears in her eyes almost made Will feel bad. "I wasn't trying to hurt anybody; I was just... trying not to hurt. He did more than 'hurt my little feelings'. He ruined my life. And I... I just don't want to hurt anymore."

Will had to shove his hands into his pockets to keep himself from embracing her as her voice broke, and a stream of tears began running down her face. He *did* feel bad now. "Look, I don't really even know you to know your whole situation or anything like that. But I know enough to say that your life isn't ruined. Look at everything you have. One of the biggest indie magazines in the nation, this nice ass apartment, your *health*. You've got a sister that loves you, and I mean... I guess you're alright looking," he lied, thinking that she was actually quite pretty. "And you're gonna talk about your life is 'ruined' just because some dude did some stupid shit? Fuck him. I guess I get that your feelings are hurt about whatever he did, but trust me, alcohol isn't the answer. Especially if you're gonna be mowing people down in your car and shit. You don't get to do whatever you want without consequences just because you're hurting. Life doesn't work like that."

For a moment, it looked as if Will's words had made an impact on Cameron. Then she took a step forward, putting them so close that they were touching.

"Kiss my ass."

Then she was gone, slamming her bedroom door behind her. Will shook his head as he pulled his phone from his pocket. He was relieved to see that Derek had returned his message.

"Jai is on her way. How did you end up with Cameron?" - Derek

"Ran into her at Donovan's." - Will

"The cop bar? What the hell was she doing at a cop bar?" -Derek.

Chapter Seven
— & —
Jai
Saturday, December 20th

Derek was looking at her. Staring, really. It took Jai a moment to fully wake, but when she did, she had to bite the inside of her lip to keep herself from breaking into a goofy grin.

"What you grinning about girl?"

"Nothing." She rolled away, turning her back to him on her bed. There was no way she was going to tell Derek what she was thinking. In the breakup with Elliott, Jai had been called many things. Needy, crazy, bitchy, you name it. So moving forward, Jai's primary goal in whatever she had going with Derek was to not be a needy, crazy bitch. What she was smiling about definitely fell into the categories of needy and crazy.

Derek wrapped his arms around her waist, pulling her back against his chest. "Alright. I'm gonna tickle the hell out of you until you tell me." He slid his hands underneath the oversized tee shirt she wore, resting them against her stomach to emphasize his threat.

"Uh uh, don't do that!" She giggled as he glided his fingers over her bare skin.

"You know what you've gotta do to get out of it, right?"

Jai wiggled out of his arms so that she could turn to face him. "Do you think we're moving too fast?" She dropped her eyes as soon as the words left her lips. *Damn. Scratch needy off the list.*

Derek raised an eyebrow, but didn't respond until he had pulled her closer, enough to press a soft kiss against her forehead. "I think you're changing the subject, but I'll go with it. Explain."

"Well," Jai tilted her head back, so that she could look into his face while she spoke. Big mistake. As soon as her eyes landed on his, she felt familiar warmth between her thighs. Happened every time. She quickly turned her gaze to a safer view, the freckles sprinkled across his nose. "I'm in your bed."

"*Sleeping*. You're in my bed because we were sleeping. That's it. And what, you don't like kicking it with me?"

Jai shook her head. "No, I love being with you, It's just... We've only really been talking for what, three months? It just feels like we got really close, really fast, and that..."

"Scares you?" Derek used a finger under her chin to tip her head up so that she was looking right into his eyes. Jai simply nodded. "So you think I'm somebody you should be scared of?" Another nod. "And why is that?"

"Well, because," Jai said, with an exaggerated roll of her eyes. How could he *not* know what she meant? "You're handsome, well-employed, not an obvious psychopath. And single. It's too good to be true, and I'm just waiting on a girlfriend or wife to jump out of the shadows and kick my ass."

Derek threw his head back to laugh. "Are you serious, Jai?"

"As a heart attack." She sat up, propping herself against the dark mahogany head board. "This all has a very 'too good to be true' vibe about it, and I just don't want to be naive about it. I don't want to assume anything."

"You don't have to. I don't have a problem with being upfront with you. For example, I had just ended a three-year long relationship the day before I met you. Because of Cameron, actually."

Jai narrowed her eyes at Derek's relaxed form. "What the hell do you mean 'because of Cameron'? I know you're not trying to say that you and she were-"

"No, I'm not saying that at all. But, my ex thought that was the case. For a few months, Cameron was my most 'critical' patient, so I was with her a lot, and any time my ex asked about my day, Cameron was naturally part of the conversation. Yeah, she and I bumped heads, but she did her best, so I would brag on her sometimes, you know?"

"Yeah, you were happy to see her making progress."

Derek threw his hands up. "Exactly! But...Jessica — that's her name— started to have a problem with it. Started asking me if I was 'really *just*' Cameron's therapist. And it wasn't the first time she accused of me of sleeping with my clients, which I take pretty personally. I would never risk my license, hell, my entire career to blur that line."

"So you broke up with her?"

96

"I had to. That jealousy shit was getting way out of hand, and I was getting sick of it. The final straw was when she threatened to 'go see' Cameron."

Jai's face immediately broke into a scowl. "Say what now? See, it's a good thing you handled it, because I would have killed her ass about my sister."

"Yeah, I know, lil' Scrappy. Cameron keeps reminding me you like to fight."

"I don't *like* to fight. People just…make it necessary sometimes."

"Necessary, huh?" Derek pulled Jai down into his arms. "You wanna talk about last night?"'

No. Jai entire mood changed. "Cameron cursed me out, then kicked me out of her apartment. What is there to talk about?"

Cameron hadn't wanted to be told that everything Will said to her, despite her displeasure with his delivery, was absolutely right. She didn't want to hear that she had a drinking problem. But Jai didn't have the emotional energy to just be quiet and sympathetic, especially when Cameron wouldn't even tell her why she was drinking again. Hell, *if* she had ever even stopped.

Nope, Cameron just wanted to go on and on about Will. Will was an asshole, Will was a jerk, Will was an asshole *and* a jerk. Never mind that *Will* had kept her ass from going to jail and gotten her home when she was in no condition to do so herself.

So Jai laid into her. And it was ugly.

"What the fuck is your problem Cameron? You really act like you're the first person in the world to get cheated on! You're not, so get over it. You want to run around talking about how Kyle fucked up your world, but guess what? Kyle isn't the one putting drinks in your hand. That's all you, Cameron.

"Stop trying to blame this bullshit on any and everybody else. You're so damned selfish. Yeah, you the accident, I get that you've been going through it, but have you thought about anybody other than yourself in the last six months? No. This drunk bullshit of yours doesn't just affect you. And you want to drink and drive *Cameron? Is that what you're telling me? With our history, you're gonna drink and drive? Do I need to remind you that our pitiful, drunk ass momma drove into oncoming traffic, with daddy in the car? Did you forget that shit Cam? Did you forget that a drunk driver hit* you? *You must*

have forgotten, because you can't be this stupid. I knew I should have kicked your ass about this shit last month.

"Jai, I-"

"No! I don't wanna hear it. What happened to you? Where is my funny, happy, energetic sister? Bring her back, because I don't know this new girl. This drunk *girl.*

"I could have died, Jai. My legs were crushed. I had to learn to walk again. My fiancé cheated on me with his ex wife, and got her pregnant. That's *what happened to that girl."*

"Sounds like a bunch of tired ass excuses to me."

"You know what, Jai? You have a lot of nerve acting like 'little miss perfect'. Are you gonna act like I didn't rescue your ass from Elliott? Like you didn't make a damn fool of yourself with Brian? And that's just this *year! I've been cleaning up behind your bullshit our whole life!"*

"Don't try to put it off on my. You're better than this shit, Cam."

"Whatever, Jai, don't try to sugarcoat anything for me. I'm good, at home, not going anywhere else tonight, so you don't have to worry about me and my 'little feelings'. You can go."

Jai almost felt bad that she had gone off on Cameron again. Almost. She couldn't understand why her twin didn't seem to get the magnitude of what she was doing to herself, and that pissed her off. Big time. The news about Angie's pregnancy didn't surprise Jai. She had been expecting that there would be more to the story, and there it was.

"You sounded really upset last night when you called me."

"Well, yeah," Jai said, tracing Derek's hairline with her fingers. "I *walked* to Cam's apartment last night because the traffic was backed up from the snow. By the time I left, there was like, an extra foot of that stuff on the ground, I wasn't walking home in that! You live around the block from Cameron."

"So you only called me because I was convenient?"

"Mmm hmm."

"And the snow was the only reason you sounded upset?"

"The only one I care to talk about right now. There's something else I'd rather do."

Jai giggled as Derek ran a hand up the back of her thigh, then gripped a handful of her butt, which was covered in a pair of his

98

boxers. "And what might that be?"

"Who told you that you could touch me like this?"

Derek wiggled his eyebrows at her as he slid his hand underneath her tee shirt, allowing it to rest just below her bare breast. "You want me to stop?"

When Jai shook her head, he moved his hand up, caressing her breast before he concentrated his thumb on the nipple, which hardened in response to his touch. Jai couldn't help the moan that escaped her throat when he pushed the shirt over her head, then replaced his fingers with his mouth. It had been a long time, more than eight months since she had been this intimate with anyone, and she had been craving this kind of touch. She shivered as Derek kissed his way up to her neck on one side, whispered "Tell me when to stop," into her ear, then kissed down the other side to give the other breast some attention. He was crazy if he thought she was going to tell him to stop.

Derek gently tugged the boxers down her legs, then returned his mouth to her, kissing a trail from her breasts to her bellybutton. Jai took in a breath as he dipped lower and lower, releasing it as a frustrated sigh when he bypassed where she *really* wanted him to plant kisses on her inner thighs. He laughed at her reaction as he spread her legs wide, and then without warning, his mouth was right where she needed it to be.

God, yes.

She squirmed underneath him, too caught up in the pleasure to be embarrassed by the gibberish that was escaping her mouth.

Oh damn!

She bit her lip as he slid a first, then second finger inside of her, pushing deep to find the elusive spot that Jai wasn't even sure she had. But nope, there it was. *Holy shit,* there it was. There. It. Was. Jai's instinctive reaction was to jerk her legs closed, but Derek locked his arm around her thigh, dragging her closer as he continued to stroke her with his fingers and tongue.

The shuddering of her legs made the entire bed shake as an orgasm wracked her body, causing her to collapse back into the pillows with a deep moan of satisfaction. She wanted to smile at Derek as he kissed his way back up to her neck, but her energy was drained.

"You ready for me to stop?"

"Uh-uh."

"Are you on birth control?"

"Mmhm."

Jai held her breath again as he entered her, inch by thick, hard, inch. This time, it was released as a *satisfied* sigh as he filled her, slowly, taking care to allow her body to adjust to him before he began to stroke. He felt good.

Damn, he feels good. How the hell does he feel so gooood?

Her breath quickened with his pace, and Jai crossed her legs around his waist, giving him permission to go deeper, and deeper, and *oh my God, what is he touching?* But it didn't matter, because even though it hurt a little, it felt *so* damn good. *Damn* it was good.

Then he was kissing her. A sweet, passionate kiss that contradicted his long, pounding strokes, but even that was good to Jai. It was all *so damn good.* She tried to tell him, but it came out as in the same nonsensical dialect as everything else she'd been trying to say. It didn't matter. He knew. He *had* to know exactly how good he was. Why else would he be wearing that cocky grin as he pulled one of her legs from his waist and hooked it over his shoulder? And how did he know that the slight pressure of his hand against her neck, keeping her in place, would take her to a whole *other* level, where she came with such intensity that she saw stars? How did he know that would happen?

When they were both spent, soaking wet with sweat even though the room had a slight chill, they collapsed together on the bed, facing each other. Derek's hand was tangled in Jai's locs, massaging her scalp as she traced her fingers in the lines of his abs.

"Hey," he said, sitting up as if he'd suddenly remembered something. "You realize you never did tell me what you were thinking about earlier?"

Jai squinted, wrinkling her brow in a bad attempt to pretend that she didn't know what he was talking about.

"Nope, don't even try it. I threatened you before, and I'll do it again. Tell me what was up, or I'm gonna tickle you until you pee on yourself, and *then* I'm going to tell everybody I know about it."

"Whatever, Derek. You aren't gon— AH!" Jai shrieked as Derek's fingers found her stomach. "Ok, ok! I'll tell you!"

Derek crossed his arms over his chest, wearing a satisfied smirk. "I'm waiting."

Jai took a deep breath.

Here goes.

"When I woke up… the first thing I saw was those gorgeous eyes of yours, then the rest of you. You were staring at me, and it kinda took my breath away. And I… I just thought that it would be… nice I guess… to wake up to that every day. I know that's crazy, because we haven't eve—"

Jai's speech was interrupted by Derek's lips against hers. She parted her lips willingly for him to slip his tongue into her mouth for yet another dizzying kiss. Jai sighed into his mouth as he pulled her close, loving the intimacy of his naked body against hers.

"Will you stop that?" He asked when he finally pulled away.

"Stop what?"

"Downplaying everything. It's ok to just feel how you feel, Jai. And if you feel like it would be nice to wake up next to me everyday, that's cool, cause guess what? I wouldn't mind waking up every day next to you.

A grin spread across Jai's face. "Well… *every* day might be a bit of stretch right now."

"Ohh, I called your bluff, huh?"

"Just a *little*," she said, holding up her pointer finger and thumb as she pinched them together.

Derek placed a kiss on her forehead, the tip of her nose, then down to her lips. "I like you, Jai. A lot. *A lot*."

"Well, Derek… I like you a lot too."

— *&* —
Cameron
Wednesday, Christmas Eve

Cameron hesitated as she pressed her fingers against the front door of Honeybee. This was unexplored territory in her relationship with her sister. For them to go four days without speaking to each other was unheard of. To be fair, none of the blame for that lied with Jai. She had reached out via text, in an attempt to break the ice, and Cameron had ignored it, holding on to the drunken logic that Jai was 'just being a bitch.'

It was all drunken logic these days, and Cameron really didn't even know what to do about that. None of her expensive education had included a course on "How to *not* be the Heartbroken, Crippled,

Drunk Girl." How the hell was she supposed to deal with this? How did she move past it? Certainly not without Jai, who was the only person in the world that she could always lean on. That was one thing Cameron definitely understood.

So, somewhere in her inebriated mind, Cameron had found enough of a hold on reality to pull herself out of bed to bathe, drink half of a pot of coffee, take a handful of ibuprofen to kill the pain in her head and legs, and *not* take a single drink that morning. And it hurt. It really freaking hurt.

Without the alcohol-induced haze, she was acutely aware of the fact that there was no saving her relationship with Kyle. After spending three years of her life loving him, the end-game of becoming a wife had slipped right through her fingers, and she didn't know what, if anything, she could have done differently. Should she have just given the whole 'side-baby' thing a chance? Maybe it was just like trying to make one last pair of jeans fit into a suitcase. Yeah, you could stuff them in there, but there was the constant fear that the zipper would pop open, spitting everything out into a disheveled pile. That would be Cameron. Forcing herself to stay in a relationship where she was always just waiting for the last blow, the one that would just spill her heart onto the floor in pieces.

But... she was in pieces anyway. There was no use denying that. Cameron didn't even feel like herself anymore, just fragments of who she used to be back when the worst thing Kyle had ever done was leave empty boxes in the pantry. Back when the streets of the city were just streets, and cars were just cars, instead of instruments of death and destruction.

Her rational mind told her that she should focus on the positives. Cameron knew that it would be wise to just hold on to the wonderful parts of life as tightly as she could. Just cling to those, instead of letting herself wander into darkness, but seriously, how? *How*? How do you just brush off two big devastating blows, delivered in the same night? How do you recover, when you're think you're past the heartbreak, only to get knocked on your ass *again*? Cameron had an answer: drink as many bottles as it took, of whatever it took, to forget.

But she knew that wasn't the right answer. Cameron was actually quite sure that choosing to self-medicate was circling the most obviously wrong choice on the test, but she was torn. The part of her that craved another shot of anesthetic begged her to just go home, and break the seal on another bottle.

She opened the door to the restaurant instead. While she still had the nerve to do it, she strode purposefully past the tables filled with customers enjoying their Christmas Eve lunches, through the doors that led to the kitchen, and right up to Jai, who seemed so occupied with not burning whatever she was cooking and barking orders to the others that it took her a moment to realize that Cameron was standing there.

Jai froze in place, and some savvy line cook had the presences of mind to slip the skillet she held from her hand, taking over the dish. From the look of trepidation on Jai's face, Cameron knew her sister was uneasy about her unannounced visit. She choked back the twinge of irrational anger she felt about being judged, deciding that she would have to be the one to break the ice.

"I'm sorry." Despite her promises to herself that she would not, under any circumstances, cry in public, Cameron's face was wet with tears as words tumbled out of her mouth. "I'm sorry for embarrassing you, and being ungrateful, and being a mess, and I don't know what to do with myself anymore Jai, and I-"

"Hush," Jai said, silencing Cameron by wrapping her arms around her neck to pull her into a hug. Cameron's knees went weak with relief. She hadn't realized just how much she missed her sister until this moment.

But it felt… hollow.

And Cameron knew exactly why. She had lied to Jai, embarrassed her, and then, when she dared to try to be a good sister and rein in her drinking, Cameron had kicked her out, in the middle of the snow. And, oh yeah, when Jai tried to reach out after that, to clear the air, she had ignored her. So Cameron wasn't exactly up for sister of the year. And yet, here Jai was, in the middle of an obviously busy time, literally providing a shoulder for Cameron to cry on.

That made her cry even harder, because she had honestly been a terrible sister. She didn't know what was going on in Jai's life, but she had been more than willing to dump her problems at her door. She allowed Jai to lead her into the office, where she pushed Cameron onto the sofa and sat beside her.

"Cam, tell me what's going on, sis." The soothing sound of Jai's voice did nothing to help the flood of tears.

"Everything," Cameron sobbed, laying her head down on Jai's lap. "Jai, I feel like I just can't get it together. I was good for like... a whole day, and then *bam* everything just went to shit again."

Jai ran a hand through Cameron's hair, twisting several soft coils around her fingers. "Sis, nobody expects you to have it all together right now, you're putting that pressure on yourself. I've told you, nobody would blame you in the least if you spent your nights watching Lifetime movies, eating ice cream, and drinking the *occasional* entire bottle of wine. It's ok to be a mess, Cam. It's the self-destructive stuff that I can't sit back and not say anything about. I love you too much for that."

Cameron's smile was weak as she gazed up at her sister. She was grateful for Jai, but she was drained, physically and emotionally.

"Listen," Jai continued, "I want you to come and stay with me."

Cameron started to protest, but Jai held up a hand, stopping her. "Just for a few days, until you're a little less in your feelings, ok? Besides, it's Christmas time! We always spend it together anyway, remember?"

"Of course I remember, I'm not senile."

"See! Then, it's settled. I'll call a cab to take you back to your place to pack enough for a week, and I'll swing by to get you after the early dinner service tonight, ok?"

Cameron shook her head as she sat up. Sure, she could argue with Jai about this, but they both knew it was pointless.

"If you say so, Jai."

"I say so! You can help me with Christmas dinner."

"Ugh, do I have to?" Cameron rolled her eyes, thinking about the disaster that had occurred last time she 'helped' with dinner.

"Be serious, Cam, you know you can't cook. *You* aren't touching the food. But you can set a beautiful table."

— *&*—
Will
Christmas Day

Merry fucking Christmas to me.

Will lounged back in his chair. As he did, he noticed that Cameron was still wearing the same grim expression she'd been wearing most of the evening. It hadn't taken him long to realize that she wasn't pleased with his presence at their Christmas dinner. In fact, she was *pissed*. He'd heard her not-that-quietly whispered question of "What the hell is *this* motherfucker doing here?" to Jai as soon as he showed up at the door.

After exchanging a quick 'What did you get me into?" look with Derek, he had followed his friend into the living room to kick back in front of the TV until a rather grumpy-looking Cameron came to retrieve them to eat dinner. Will had been skeptical about sharing a meal with Cameron, but when Derek explained that Jai was the head chef at Honeybee, there was no way he was passing up a chance to see what she could do with a traditional Christmas dinner.

When his grueling overnight shift in the ambulance was over, Will had gone home, showered, then collapsed into the bed until it was time to go to Jai's. He hadn't been greeted very warmly by Cameron when she answered the doorbell, but even her lack of hospitality hadn't been enough to overshadow the delicious food. Now he was full, satisfied, and ready for a nap.

Jai and Derek had left the table shortly after clearing their lightly-prepared plates, disappearing into the back of the apartment like horny teenagers. Will turned his attention to Cameron, who was quiet, staring down at her half-eaten plate. Even with no makeup, her hair undone and brushed away from her face, Cameron was ridiculously pretty with her smooth cocoa skin and big brown eyes, and those sexy ass lips. If he had to guess, her breasts were probably perfect handfuls. He would have loved to put his estimation to the test, if only she weren't such a bi—

"You know they set us up, right?"

Will lazily brought his gaze back up to her face, which was no longer pulled into a scowl. She actually wore a hint of a smile, like she knew exactly where his eyes had been, and possibly didn't mind.

"Set us up?" Will took a long sip from his water glass, watching Cameron finish a forkful of sweet potatoes before responding.

"Well, my sister seems to think that I dislike you so much because I secretly want to sleep with you."

Will grinned as he placed his glass back down on the table. "Is that true?" He nearly laughed aloud at Cameron's obvious struggle not to smile.

"You're a handsome guy Will, but no. I don't like you because I just don't like you."

Well, that wasn't what he expected her to say, but not exactly surprising. "Because of the...uh... incident, last weekend?"

"Bingo."

Will nodded, pushing his plate back on the table so that he could rest his elbows there. "I guess I could see that. Derek told me I may have been a little hard on you."

"Humph. A little? You crossed a line! Despite the fact that you played a part in saving my life, you don't even know me. You had no right."

She really doesn't get it, Will thought as he blew out a breath. "I don't need to know you to see that you were acting recklessly, and putting yourself and others in danger."

Cameron rolled her eyes as she pushed a hand through her hair. "Here you go again with this after-school special stuff."

"I know you think I'm just on some self-righteous bullshit, but listen for a second. Did Derek tell you that I have a daughter?"

"No," she replied, resting her chin in her hands. "Why aren't you with her? It's Christmas."

"She's across the country, with her mother and grandparents. But that's beside the point. When Kelly was ten years old, she got hit by a drunk driver while she was walking across the street." Will swallowed heavily. He hated talking about this, but he knew it would get her attention better than lecturing.

The bored expression immediately dropped from Cameron's face as she sat up.

"Middle of the afternoon, some bored soccer mom decided to get 'turnt up' before she joined the pick-up line and nearly killed my baby." Will shook his head, unsuccessfully trying to not relive the experience of hearing that his little girl was hurt.

Cameron reached forward, placing a hand on Will's knee. "I'm so sorry. Is she ok now?"

"God was looking out for her. The recovery process was slow and exhausting, especially for a kid. But she got through it. She's a tough girl."

"I'm sure you had a great support system in place in for her."

Will looked up, making sure that his eyes connected with Cameron's. "So do you. Derek was her physical therapist, that's how

106

we met. He helped make my baby whole again."

"That's... amazing."

"Yeah, it was. But do you see now why drinking and driving pisses me off so bad? Kelly is good now, but it took damn near two years for her life to be somewhat back to normal. That shit doesn't just affect *you*. You could be fucking up someone else's life."

Cameron gave a slight nod before she looked away, staring down at her hands. *Shit*. He wasn't trying to make her sad again. He took another long sip of water, almost wishing it was a beer, but for Cameron's sake, Jai had declared it a 'dry' Christmas. He didn't even drink anymore, not since Kelly's accident, but he definitely could have used one before dealing with an emotional woman.

"Hey," he said, waiting for Cameron to look up before he continued, "You've got way too much going for yourself to fuck up your life."

"Who says I'm doing that?"

Will raised an eyebrow, then nodded his head in the direction of where Derek and Jai had disappeared.

"Ah, I see. *Jai* says so." Cameron pulled her mouth into a line, then released a heavy breath as she sat back. Tears were in her eyes when she spoke again. "She's right."

"So do something about it."

Cameron shrugged. "I wish it were that easy. A lot has happened in the last six months. Too much to pretend like everything is the same, like it's perfect, when it's clearly not. It's not ok. *I'm* not ok. I keep hearing that I should be glad for a second chance, but it really feels like a nightmare I can't get out of. I just wanna wake up." She snatched a napkin from the table, using it to dry her face.

Feeling helpless, Will stood, walking away from the table to put some distance between he and Cameron. He may not like her very much, but it didn't change the fact that he hated to see one cry.

"Maybe you should talk to someone," Will said as he grabbed his plate to take into the kitchen.

"That's what I'm doing, I'm talking to you."

Will laughed. "I'll have you even more fucked up talking to me."

"So you think I'm messed up too?"

"Hey, those are your words, not mine. Seriously though, Kelly had to talk to a child psychologist after the accident. It helped a lot.

Got her past the depression, the anger, all of that. It would help you."
After Kelly's accident, she'd had the same sad, distant look in her eyes
that Cameron wore. Even when her face was smiling, she was
pretending to be happy, the eyes always gave it away.

Cameron stood, stretching before she brought her own used
dishes to the sink. "I'll think about it," she said as she began to rinse
her glass.

"Don't just think about it, do it."

"Ok."

"Hey," Will said, gently pulling her arm until she was facing
him. "I'm serious. You say you're ready to get on with your life, then
do it," he insisted.

"I said I would." Cameron leaned back against the counter.

Will placed his hands on either side of her, trapping her in
place. "I'm gonna bug the shit out of you until you do."

"You're annoying as hell," Cameron said, placing her hands on
his chest in a futile effort to push him away.

"I've been called worse." He stepped back, giving her room to
leave the kitchen without even bothering to say goodbye. Chuckling,
he went back to cleaning his dishes. He wasn't sure why he pushed so
hard with Cameron, other than it feeling like the right thing to do. He
just hoped it would get through to her.

Feeling movement in the room, he looked behind him to see
that Cameron had returned, with her hands clenched nervously behind
her back. "I, uh... just wanted to say thank you."

"For what?"

"For listening and not babying me. And for not yelling at me
this time," she added, smiling. It was real smile, one that transformed
her face so much that Will had to blink to make sure he wasn't
imagining it. Cameron was gorgeous.

"Uh, yeah," Will stammered. "I'm sorry about last week. I
went a little too far."

"It's ok. Especially now that I know about your daughter. I
would be upset too. I *should* be upset, because someone did the same
thing to me."

Yes!

"So you get it now?"

Cameron nodded. "Yeah, I think I do. Again, thanks."

"Hey, I think you just needed a friend."

"Is that what we are now?"

"Probably better than hating each other." Will extended his hand towards her. "Friends?"

Cameron smiled as she returned his gesture.

"Yeah. Friends."

— & —

Jai
Wednesday, December 31st

I'm going to kill him.

Jai slowly stood up from the toilet, cringing as her panties touched the now hyper-sensitive area between her legs. Swallowing the urge to cry from the pain, she ran a mental inventory of every unprotected sexual encounter she'd had with Derek since the first time. She shook her head at herself when she ran out of fingers to count on.

"Stupid, stupid, stupid. Stupid!" She ranted in the bathroom mirror, angrily flipping the fixture on the faucet. "Raw sex, Jai? Really? Are you serious right now? Could you have been any more idiotic? No, you couldn't have. Stupid!" She dried her hands and exited her private bathroom, still cursing herself. She needed to get to her phone, and make an appointment for an emergency visit with her gynecologist.

Jai had only taken a few steps back into her office when she realized Brian was sitting at her desk, with a questioning look on his face. She blew out a heavy breath. Before she had embarrassed herself by coming on to him, she would have been able to talk to him about this, but now that things were all weird, he was one of the last people she wanted to look at.

Jai focused on keeping her expression guarded as she faced him from across the office. "Brian, please make it quick. What do you want?"

He raised an eyebrow, seemingly surprised by her abruptness. "Well, you know I told you a few weeks ago that equipment was coming up missing? It's still happening, so I want to talk to you about insta—"

"Fine. It's fine," she interrupted. "Whatever you wanna do, it's fine, ok?" Jai plastered on a smile, despite the deafening throb of pain between her legs. She just needed to get him out of here. "You're the manager, you can decide. So, was that all?"

"Uh… Jai? Are you—?"

"I'm fine; I just need you to go." She was trying not to scream at him, but his presence seemed to be intensifying her distress.

"Um, ok… " Brian stood, still eyeing her with suspicion as he turned to leave. "I'll just send you any—"

"Yeah, whatever, bye!" She pushed him the last few inches out of the door, locking it behind him. Dashing back to the desk, she flung open the top drawer to receive her cell phone. She *had* to get in to see someone today.

— & —
Wednesday Afternoon

"You thought you had a STD?"

"It's really not that damn funny, Dr. Kim," Jai mumbled, rolling her eyes at the laughter from her gynecologist. She was embarrassed that she had been so dramatic about this whole ordeal, but relieved that Derek hadn't passed a disease to her. "Al I knew was that I started having sex with him last week. This week, I sat down to pee and felt like someone had doused me in gasoline and thrown a lit match at my crotch. I can admit that I may have overreacted a little."

"Oh please," Dr. Kim responded, still laughing. "You came in here ready to kill that boyfriend of yours over a UTI we've been battling for a year."

"I thought we got rid of that." Jai crossed her arms, guiltily remembering that she never finished the last round of antibiotics, opting to just stop once she felt better.

Dr. Kim shrugged. "So did I, but it seems to be back. Have you had any major changes in diet, sexual activity, changed your soap or laundry detergent?"

"No to the major changes in diet, yes to the change in sexual activity, and yes to the change in laundry detergent." Jai thought back to Cameron's insistence that she try the same lavender-scented organic crap she used for her own clothes.

"Well, there you go. These things just happen; it's an unfortunate part of being a woman. We'll get you an antibiotic, something stronger this time, and see if we can get rid of this thing for good. You'll be just fine, and no need to kill your boyfriend."

"I'm just glad I decided to call and get checked out first. I started to ride by his job and slash his tires."

Jai laughed at the horrified look on her sweet, quiet doctor's face. "Relax, Dr. Kim, I'm just playing. I don't mess with people's property. I definitely would have kicked his ass though."

Not looking very convinced, Dr. Kim handed Jai the prescription and began giving instructions. "This is for 5 days. I want you to make sure you take them *all*, ok?"

Chapter Eight
— & —
Derek
Thursday, January 1st

Derek should have stayed home. He *knew* he shouldn't have agreed to this meeting. *He knew it.* Yet, there he was, sitting across from Jessica at a table while she cried her eyes out over... whatever the hell Derek had done this time, even though they were no longer together. He shook his head. Jessica was an expert at turning on the waterworks to get her way, but not this time.

He shot an apologetic smile to the group of women eyeing him from the next table, no doubt wondering exactly how much of a jerk he had been to make such a pretty girl cry so hard. He could practically see the wheels turning in their heads as they scowled in his direction. Still, he wasn't giving in. No matter what Jessica did, or threatened to do, he would offer no apologies, no comfort, nothing. Once she realized that tears weren't working, she would switch tactics, and maybe then she would finally get to the *real* reason why she had called and asked Derek to have lunch.

Derek gave a quiet snort of laughter when he spotted her peeking through a break in her fingers to see how he was reacting to her little show. Seemingly unsatisfied with his response, she dropped her hands from her face and whipped out a compact mirror. Derek watched, amused, as she carefully dried any remnants of tears, making sure to leave what he knew was meticulously applied makeup in place. Everything about Jessica was contrived.

That's why Jai was such a breath of fresh air.

After spending three years of his life with her, Derek knew that Jessica devoted several hours of her day, every day, to her appearance. She thrived on strict regimens at the gym, countless jars of face creams, and he had been unfortunate enough to stumble upon a collection of fake hair that could have easily handled that big oil spill in the gulf. It was insane.

Jai, on the other hand, was just… Jai. She ran in the mornings if she felt like it, washed her face with whatever she showered with, and slathered herself from head to toe with whatever scented shea butter she felt like using that morning. She was effortlessly pretty, and just… simple. He didn't have to worry about her getting mad that he had forgotten the obscure anniversary of the first time they saw a red car together. There would never be tears, and accusations of cheating because he sent her pink roses instead of red. That crazy life of walking on eggshells ended with Jessica. Sweet, beautiful, laid-back Jai was exactly what he needed.

"—Derek, are you even listening to me?"

"No," he replied, not bothering to camouflage the boredom in his voice. "Can you get to the point, Jessica? I can think of about a thousand things I'd rather be doing right now."

Derek let out an exasperated sigh as Jessica's hand fluttered up to her chest. "How can you be so cruel to me, Derek, after three years? I've always treated you with nothing b—"

"Jessica… The point, please?"

Anger flashed in Jessica's eyes as she dropped her hand. "Fine," she spat. "I wanted to talk to you in person, to see if you were finally going to stop being such an as—"

"Bye Jessica." Derek tossed down enough cash to cover their bill and a tip, then pushed his chair back from the table and stood to leave. This was the other thing. The childish name calling she resorted to when she wasn't getting her way. *That* shit drove him up the wall, and it was the quickest route to get him pissed off. The difference was that now, he didn't have to put up with it. He could just walk away.

"*Wait*!" Jessica jumped up, latching herself onto his arm before he could walk away. "I'm sorry, ok? I asked you here to see if we could work this out. We were together for three years, that's not the type of thing you just throw away."

Derek wrenched himself free of her grasp before responding. "No, we can't work this out. Three years was plenty to see that I'm not the guy for you. The jealously, the lack of maturity, the… the *hair*. I just can't deal, Jessica."

"So you think you're just Mr. Perfect? You never did any wrong, huh?" She asked, an ugly expression masking her delicate features.

"I never said that. I'm just telling you what I don't want to deal with."

"Good. Because I put up with plenty of bullshit from you as well."

Derek fought the urge to ask her to name the 'bullshit', but he knew that was only going to lead to an even bigger scene than they had already made. "Look Jessica, we both have plenty of complaints about the other, so I don't really see why you think there's anything to salvage."

"I get that, but maybe we can go to counseling, or—"

"No."

Jessica propped her hands on her hips. "No?"

"That's what I said."

"Why not?" she persisted.

Because I just don't want to, damn.

"Because I'm seeing someone."

Jessica gasped, recoiling as if she had been slapped. Derek shook his head, admonishing himself for his choice of answer. It would have been easier to just go with "Nah, I'm good."

"I *knew* it," she said, jabbing a finger dangerously close to his face. "How long have you been fucking her? Was it before we broke up? It's that 'Cameron' bitch isn't it?"

"I'm not about to do this with you Jessica."

Before he could turn to leave, he felt the full impact of a drink, glass and all, being thrown into his face.

God. Please give me the strength not to choke this woman. I don't want to go to jail today.

Derek took the deepest breath he could as he wiped the cold water from his face, willing himself not to react. Jessica had her hands clutched over her mouth, as if she had surprised even herself by resorting to drink throwing.

"Derek... I—"

"No. *No.* What the hell is wrong with you? Throwing drinks? Do you think you're on a reality show or something?"

"De—"

"No. *Hell* no. I said I wasn't gonna do this shit with you, and I'm not."

Derek tuned out her pleas as he stalked out of the restaurant to his truck, ignoring the open stares of the other patrons. Relieved that

Jessica hadn't followed him outside, he took a moment to massage his aching temples, hoping to alleviate the pounding headache that had developed from the encounter. When he pulled out of the parking lot, he headed straight for Honeybee.

He needed his fresh air.

When he walked into Honeybee's sleek, stainless steel clad kitchen, he was greeted by the sight of Jai leaning over a counter as she checked off items on a list. All around her, the staff moved in organized chaos as they did their prep work for the dinner service. But as usual, Jai was surrounded by an aura of peace.

Derek needed to touch her, so he moved closer, wrapping his arms around her waist. To his surprise, she immediately stiffened, moving away from his touch.

"Damn, will you cut it out?" Jai asked, tossing her pen onto the counter as she turned around. "I've told y— Oh, Derek!" Her scowl was replaced by the beautiful smile he had been thinking about all morning, and she threw her arms around his neck to hug him. "Sorry for snapping at you. I thought you were someone who doesn't have permission to be *all up on me* like that."

Derek's frowned. It only took him a second to figure out who Jai had assumed he was.

"Don't give me that look, I know," Jai said, running her hand along his stubbled chin in a soothing gesture. "That's why I reacted like that."

Shaking his head, Derek looped his arms around her waist again, bending so that he could place a kiss against her earlobe. He grinned when she pressed her body closer in response, tilting her head to the side to expose her neck. "Tell me to kick his ass, and I'll do it. No questions asked," he mumbled into her chin.

"I don't think there's a need for all of that." Jai grabbed a handful of Derek's collar. "Why is your shirt all damp?"

Derek sighed, nuzzling his face into her neck. "Long, annoying story."

"I've got a little time, lover boy. Come to my office."

She beckoned with a finger and Derek followed, enjoying the view of her hips swinging back and forth as he followed her out of the kitchen. Jai glanced back, shooting him a smile that sent heat rushing to his crotch. As soon as the door closed behind them, he locked it. She shrieked when he picked her up, gently pressing her back into the wall.

Derek groaned as she wrapped her legs around his waist, crossing them at the ankles. "Come to my place tonight?" he asked, tilting her chin up to place a soft kiss against her lips.

"You know I can't, babe. Remember, my little issue..."

"So?" He kissed her again, slipping his tongue into her mouth to taste her. "I just want you close. Is that ok?"

He felt a now-familiar surge of happiness as Jai bit down on her bottom lip, something she did when she was trying not break into a goofy grin.

"In that case, yes," she said, running her fingers over his hair. "Now tell me why you're wet."

Derek sighed. "Jessica threw a drink in my face at lunch."

He cursed his decision to not change his shirt when Jai's expression went from sweet to annoyed. "Jessica, as in your ex with the jealousy problem?"

"Yes."

"A drink, as in... a glass, ice, all of that?"

"Yes."

"Lunch, as in... you sat down to eat a meal with her?"

"Yes."

Jai uncrossed her legs and pushed him away, indicating that she wanted to be let down. "Derek, there is so much wrong with that, that I don't even know where to start."

Shit. Now Jai was mad too. Derek took a step back, allowing Jai to put her feet back on the ground. Before she could walk away, he grabbed her hand, coaxing her closer. "Hey, come on now. It was just lunch, babe."

"Yeah, but why?"

Yeah, why? Derek frowned. He really didn't know why, other than the fact that she'd been calling and texting for a week, begging to meet. "I... I don't know. She said she just wanted to talk. I guess I felt like I owed it to her."

"Of course you did," Jai said, rolling her eyes. "I bet she wanted to 'talk' about getting back to together, didn't she?"

"How—"

"Because I know how women like her operate. I'm sure she has a whole bag of little manipulative tricks that work on you like magic. She's had three years to perfect it."

116

Derek shook his head. "Give me some credit Jai, I'm not an idiot. I recognized her bullshit as soon as she started. She got mad that I wasn't going for it, hence the drink in my face."

"I'm not suggesting that you're *stupid*, per se, but… ok, take Kyle, for example. You know, Cam's former fiancé? I'm sure he never thought that he would step out on Cameron, especially not with an ex. But he didn't shut it down when he should have, and you see how that ended up? I'm not trying to tell you what to do; I just want you to be mindful that you don't end up like him."

"Like him?"

"With my hands around your neck because you couldn't keep your ex off of your di—"

"Whoa," Derek chuckled nervously, remembering that one stupid night, when he and Jai had broken up for those few hours. "Trust me, Jessica and I will *never* happen again, ok?"

Jai still looked skeptical, so Derek wrapped his arms around her waist again, pulling her into a hug. "Look, woman. You are the *only* person on my mind. If that changes, which I doubt will be any time soon, I'll let you know. I'm not that dude, Jai. Ok?"

"Ok. But just kno—"

He interrupted her with another kiss. "My place, tonight, when you get off, ok?"

"Mmmhmm."

— & —
Jai
Saturday, January 3

"Mmmm. God, Derek that feels *so* good."

"You like that?"

"*Mmmhmm.* You take such good care of me. Thank you."

Jai closed her eyes, trying to relax as Derek continued the stretch on her aching knees. "I know these tendonitis flare ups are no joke. I just want you to feel better."

Leaning back into the pillows, she groaned as he moved down to her ankles, encouraging her to rotate them. The pain was so intense that she felt sick to her stomach, but she knew it was helping to loosen the stiffness in her joints. Waking up, she had barely been able to move, so she was glad that she had accepted Derek's offer to stay overnight on Friday as well.

Derek lifted her leg, placing a kiss against her pedicured toes. "Babe… I know you don't like taking pills, but I think you should take one of your anti-inflammatories. It'll help a lot."

"Can you get them for me?" Jai asked, after a heavy sigh. "They're in my purse, in your living room. And grab my antibiotics for me too, please?"

He smiled. "Good girl. Coming right up."

Jai playfully rolled her eyes at him as he sauntered out of the room, clad in nothing but boxers after his morning shower. Despite her state of discomfort, she felt a surge of arousal. Physically, Derek was perfect, but that's not what had her hot and bothered that morning. She was more enthralled by how naturally he seemed to settle into the role of caretaker. With Elliot, Jai had become accustomed to providing attention, not receiving it, so being tended to was quite refreshing.

I could get used to this.

Maybe. She couldn't get too comfortable. Not this soon. Just four months had passed since she met Derek, and they had only been seeing each other *officially* for two. Jai pushed thoughts of the future with Derek out of her mind, forcing herself to be content with the happiness of the present. She liked him very much, and based on his actions, she was confident he liked her too. For now, just that was enough.

"Jai?" She looked up as he walked back into the room, a glass of water in one hand and her pill bottles in the other. He wore a concerned look on his face that made Jai sit up a little straighter as she waited on him to finish.

Sitting down at her feet, he held up the bottle of antibiotics. "Is this what they gave you for the UTI?"

"Yeah, Cipro. I've been taking it since Wednesday, so… three days now. Why?"

Derek closed his eyes, pushing out a breath laced with frustration.

"Derek, you're scaring me. What's going on?"

"Jai… did you read the paperwork they gave you at the pharmacy before you started taking these?"

"I glanced at it," she said, shrugging. "But, it's just an antibiotic; they all say the same thing."

"Not all, babe." He held up the bottle again. "These have a

black label warning for people with tendonitis. It weakens your tendons, causes your flare ups to be even worse, increases your chances of a tendon rupture. Your doctor absolutely should *not* have prescribed these to you."

"It was my gynecologist, she doesn't even know about the tendonitis. My wrists and hands aren't really part of her concern. Besides, the major stuff listed in those side effects is super rare… Right?"

Derek shook his head, laying a hand on her knee. "This isn't one of those times. I know about this because I've worked with several patients who've had their tendons nearly destroyed because of this stuff. No, it's not definite that you'll have the same experience, but we can't take that chance. Don't take anymore of these. Call your doctor and have them give you something else."

Jai sat back, waiting on him to start laughing at his prank, but his expression remained tense. Her eyes began to well as she thought about the implications of what he was saying. *Tendons nearly destroyed.* That couldn't happen to her. How would she cook?

"So, this flare up. It's the worst one I've ever had. Do you think…?"

"It's possible, but I can't say for sure." He eased himself further onto the bed, so that he was sitting beside her. "We'll just keep an eye on it, ok?"

Jai nodded, too distracted by her own thoughts to form a response.

"Hey," Derek used a finger to gently tip her chin in his direction, forcing her to look at him. "I'm sorry I scared you." He leaned in, placing a kiss at the corner of her mouth. "I don't want you to stress yourself out about this, but it is something to take seriously. I'm just glad you're only three days in. Maybe you'll never have any issues."

"This… this can't be happening." Jai's voice cracked as her tears broke free. "What if I ca—"

"Don't do that. I didn't tell you for you to freak out, I told you so you would be informed, ok?" He kissed her again, weaving his fingers into her locs. "You're gonna be ok, baby. I promise."

"You can't promise something like that, Derek."

"The hell I can't," he said, so adamantly that Jai laughed. "There's that beautiful smile again. That's what I wanna see."

"Yeah, you say that *after* you drop a bomb on me." Jai crossed her arms, pursing her lips into a fake pout.

"Would you have preferred that I not say anything?"

She unfolded her arms, draping them over his shoulders. "Of course not. I'm glad you did. I told you, you take good care of me."

"That's kind of what you're supposed to do for people you care about."

Jai only grinned in response, using one hand to dry her face. *Can't get too comfortable.*

— & —
Cameron
Friday, January 16th

Cameron knew she was making her uncomfortable. Still, she didn't say a word. She simply stared at the terrified woman sitting in front of her. She almost felt a little sorry for her. *Almost.* She knew that this woman was just the 'fall-guy' for this epic mistake from the printing office. The sweet, pretty blonde across from her probably had very little to do with the fact that the pages were numbered incorrectly, the text was crooked, and many of the photographs were cut off in the wrong place. But, someone had to pay for it.

"Ms. Taylor… are you going to say anything?"

Cameron's eyes narrowed. "What do you propose I say? Do you want me to say this *isn't* a piece of shit?" She tossed the faulty magazine across the desk. "I can't believe you even sent this to me. Did it not occur to anyone at your office that maybe it would be a good idea to correct this before I saw it? Did you think I wouldn't look at this? What if I hadn't? What if I had simply, I don't know, trusted the people I paid a shit ton of money to get this right to *actually get it right*? This is a big deal. The proceeds from these sales are supposed to go towards helping people, and the people who posed for these pictures are depending on that. Do you know how many copies we'll sell with these kinds of errors?"

"I—"

Cameron slapped the magazine, causing the blonde to jump. "*None.* We would sell none, and my magazine gets a reputation as a producer of shittily edited trash. Do you know what Sugar & Spice absolutely *doesn't* produce?"

"I—"

"*Trash*. I don't put out trash for public consumption and call it a magazine. So you take that piece of crap back to your boss and get it fixed. This issue is supposed to be ready to sell in less than a month, in conjunction with the web launch. Get. It. Fixed. And I want it done, like, *yesterday*. No excuses." Cameron cut her eyes back to her computer screen.

"Ms. Tayl—"

"Why are you still here?"

"I just wanted to apologize, on behalf of—"

Cameron held up a hand, halting the hollow apology. "You think I want, or need to hear this? I don't. I just need your company to do what I paid them to do, which was produce a quality product. You're dismissed. Go fix my magazine and stop wasting my time."

She sighed as the woman darted out of the office, leaving the proof copy of the magazine on the desk. Cameron was exhausted by the entire encounter, and wished she had gone with the other, slightly more expensive printing company. Maybe they would have been more competent. Needing to cleanse her brain of the memory of the butchered project, she opened the file containing the pictures from the shoot on her computer.

Rashad had really done a beautiful job. Even though his personality grated on her nerves sometimes, she had to admit that he was talented. It was why she kept him around, even after the whole 'trying to sleep with her sister' thing. As she clicked her way through the pictures, she admired the fun vibe that the bright, neon colors had given the entire project. If she could get the printing company to deliver, she was sure that she would be able to cut nice big checks to each of the charities.

Cameron slowed when she neared the end of the images. These were the ones she had been roped into posing for, with Derek and Will. She was glad that she did.Those pictures, along with the interview her team had talked her into giving, would create a powerful impact. Even though the idea had been thought of before the accident, the narrative fit nicely with the "Live Savers" theme of the issue.

Her therapist, a woman named Michelle, had been the one to convince her to submit candid shots of her recovery process to include with the story, which would be placed in the front of the feature as an introduction. None of *those* images were pretty. They were really,

really ugly. But, for a while, that had been her reality. It was all part of her story, and even though she honestly wanted to vomit at the thought of people seeing her so 'undone', she had to go through with it. If there was a chance that it would convince even one person to stay off of the road if they weren't sober, it had to be done.

After her impromptu talk with Will on Christmas, Cameron couldn't get him, or his daughter, out of her head. Hearing his story, she had a ton of questions, none of which she'd been bold enough to ask. She was ashamed of herself really, thinking back to her actions the night he pulled her out of that bar. But, she reminded herself, she couldn't dwell on that. She had to work on doing, and being, better. That had started with sobriety.

Cameron never knew what she would hear, see, or remember that would kick her back down into the emotional trenches, but between Michelle and Jai, it usually only took a middle-of-the-night phone call to get her grounded enough that she wouldn't act on the impulse to drink. Not that the impulse wasn't there.

She had grudgingly sold her entire wine collection, along with the contents of her home bar to Honeybee, so the thought of having to stop what she was doing, get dressed, and drive to a store usually killed the smaller urges. The desire to possess a coveted 'one month sober' token covered everything in-between. Things were going slow, but it was steady. Cameron was *thriving* on steady.

"Knock-knock."

Cameron looked up from her computer. "Will? Hi." She forced herself to conceal the happiness in her voice at the sight of him in her doorway. She hadn't seen him since Christmas, but he'd stuck to his promise to 'bug the shit out of her' by texting her borderline crazy messages multiple times a day until she confirmed that she was seeing a therapist. After that, his correspondence had decreased to once weekly, to see how she was doing.

She shared this information with Michelle, who had immediately asked about nature of her relationship with Will. Of course, Cameron was quick to deny that there was anything other than friendship there. Will was blatantly handsome, in a you'd-have-to-be-blind-not-to-notice kind of way. And his body? Goodness gracious, Cameron would usually have a hard time forcing herself to not stare.

But, after the nightmare situation with Kyle, men, even handsome ones, were not even on her radar. What she needed from

Will was exactly what he'd offered: friendship. And she was glad to have it.

When he didn't say anything, Cameron grew uncomfortable, self-consciously smoothing down her hair. "What, Will? Why are you just staring?"

"Oh," he said, flinching as if she had surprised him. "I'm sorry, it's just... you look so different. Happier. It's a good look."

Cameron blushed, unsure what to make of the compliment. "Um, thanks. I *am* happier." Her eyes fell on the error-ridden magazine on the desk. "In general, that is. Look at this," she said, holding the magazine toward him. He closed the distance between the door and the desk to take the magazine from her, remaining standing as he flipped through it.

"Oh. This is...."

"A mess," Cameron finished for him. "I know. I'm just hoping that they don't disappoint me with the next draft. I may just flip out." She dropped her head, using her fingers to massage her temples.

"Hey, don't even dwell on that. I need you in a good mood."

Cameron looked up, raising an eyebrow. "Huh?"

"I want you to come to a basketball game with me."

"Ohh. Uh... Will, I'm not really a sports kinda girl."

Will laughed. "You don't have to be. You'll have a good time, I promise. Come on."

"What, right now?"

"Yeah, now."

Cameron shook her head. "I can't. I have to be here for at least another few hours."

"My bad," Will said, lifting his hands. "I thought you were the boss, I didn't realize you had to have permission to leave."

Cameron sucked her teeth. "Really, you're gonna do that?"

"Will it make you turn off your computer and come to this game? It's quitting time."

Glancing at the clock, she sighed. She hadn't even realized that the end of the day had come so soon. "What kind of basketball game starts at 5pm anyway?"

"You'll see when we get there. Besides, the game doesn't start at five; it starts at 6:30. Did you drive today?"

"No, I used a car service," Cameron responded as she shut her computer down. "Why? And why are you here now if the game isn't until after six?"

Will grinned. "Because, I'm gonna give you a ride home so you can change into something a little more casual."

"What's wrong with what I'm wearing?" Cameron asked, frowning down at her pencil skirt and silk blouse.

Holding out his hand, Will helped her up from her chair, allowing her to grab her purse before leading her out of the door. "We don't want anyone to know that you're not a 'sports kinda girl'."

— & —
Will
Friday Night

"Go! *Go!* Wait a minute; she can't do that, can she? Will, can she do that? Foul! She just elbowed her! Foul! Foul! That's right, isn't it? That was a foul!"

Will exchanged an amused glance with one of the other parents.

Not a sports kinda girl, my ass.

Cameron was more into Kelly's high school basketball game than most of the parents there. It had only taken a brief explanation of the rules for her to jump right in, rooting for his daughter like Kelly was her own.

Will had assumed from their short conversations that Cameron would benefit from meeting his daughter. At 16, Kelly was completely recovered from the accident six years ago, and thriving as a teenager. Her only physical reminders were a few faint scars, which she proudly wore as a survivor. Emotionally, she was probably more grounded than most kids her age, most likely due to the years of therapy.

In his head, Cameron would have sat through the game with her eyes glued to her Smartphone. Will was surprised, and pleased, to see that wasn't the case.

At her apartment, she'd changed into jeans, an oversized hoodie that he suspected belonged to her former fiancé, and a pair of pristine running shoes. There had been a moment, after she divulged that she had purchased the shoes the day before her accident, where the look in her eyes made him think that she might slip down into her feelings. But, she shook her head, tossed her shoulders back and smiled, asking if he was ready to go.

He was proud of her. Already, she was different than the sad girl he drug home from a bar last month. If this was the real her, he was looking forward to seeing more.

Cameron sat down, pulling Will's cardboard tray of nachos from his hands. "I *never* eat stuff like this. I'm sure I'm gonna regret this tomorrow, but it looks so good!" She shoved a few of the cheese-drenched chips into her mouth, licking the excess from her fingers before returning the tray to him.

"Why not? Are you one of those all-organic, health food nuts?"

"Guilty as charged," she admitted with a grin. "I was even vegan for a while, but I missed Jai's cooking too much to stick to that. I'm just glad she buys organic for Honeybee. It's not even just the fact that I'm not even sure that processed goop is *actually* cheese though. I have to watch what I eat to keep my weight in check, especially since I'm not as mobile as I used to be. I've already gained way too much since the accident."

Will lifted an eyebrow. He considered saying something to counter her comment about her weight, but quickly decided against it. There was no way he was getting roped into a body conversation with a woman. But what if by *not* saying anything, he inadvertently confirmed that she was 'fat'?

Shit.

"Cameron, stop playing. You know you look good."

"Nobody asked you," she teased, bumping his shoulder with hers. "I'm not that concerned about it though. I know it will come off once I'm cleared to start running again."

She turned her attention back to the game, which was in the final seconds, just in time to see Kelly being fouled by the same opponent as before. Just like that, Cameron was on her feet again, screaming at the referee.

Cameron was full of surprises.

Chapter Nine
— & —
Jai
Thursday January 22nd

"So I've got a surprise for you!"

Jai put down her fork, waiting on her sister to finish. She knew if she egged her on, Cameron would purposely stall, or worse, keep the news to herself.

"You remember a few days ago, when you told me you were thinking about doing a little intimate event, to celebrate Honeybee's two year anniversary?"

"Of course."

"Well," she paused to take a sip of her water, "I've been thinking."

Jai's eyes grew wide. "Cam, you are *not* gonna take this over, and turn it into—"

"It's not like that, I promise! I'm being good, just hear me out."

"Ok," Jai said, her eyebrow lifted in disbelief. "But I'm serious Cam. A *small* event."

"I know. But, a small event doesn't have to mean a small celebration. I want to do a story on Honeybee for the magazine."

Jai's face lit up with excitement. "Are you serious Cameron?!"

"Of course," she said, reaching across the table to grab Jai's hand. "I don't know why I didn't think about it before! I don't know you didn't *ask* me before."

Jai shrugged, dropping her eyes to the table. "I mean, Honeybee is just a local thing, Sugar & Spice is like… big time, you know?"

"No… I don't." Cameron frowned. "Honeybee is a big freaking deal, Jai. Just because it's local doesn't make it irrelevant. Hell, the Life Savers shoot was all local people, but look at the buzz

126

it's gotten!"

"Well yeah, but those people are impor—"

"Jai!"

Jai rolled her eyes before bringing them back up to meet Cameron's.

"You know you *have* to do this now, right?" Cameron asked. "It's not an option. You need to see just how 'big time' Honeybee really is."

"Don't get me wrong, I know that the restaurant is successful, it's just that—"

"It's just that you're letting Elliot back in your head again."

Letting out a frustrated sigh, Jai released Cameron's hand. "Nobody is thinking about him."

"Yeah right. You never lacked confidence in *anything* until his ass. You've always been good at everything you tried, while I have to work at it. But you started dating him, and he had you dieting, wearing a bunch of makeup, and doubting yourself, things you never did before him."

"He just wanted me to better myself," Jai said defensively, crossing her arms over her chest.

"Girl, you don't even believe that yourself. That's why even though he didn't want you to, you took the chance and opened Honeybee. And you see how he reacted behind *that*. What kind of man doesn't want his woman to be successful, Jai? That's why he tried to tear you down. He saw that fire in you, and it was bigger than his, so he had to try to put it out. And you internalized that bullshit. That's why you're sitting here referring to *your* restaurant as 'just a little local thing', when this place is packed out all day every day."

Feeling her anger deflate, Jai dropped her arms back to her sides. She didn't want to admit it, but Cameron was right. Her full restaurant and the steadily growing figure in her bank account told a much different story from how she perceived her own success. Even though she knew Honeybee was popular, she had a hard time reconciling that with the feeling that she should be further, have done more by now.

She could admit that it was silly. A successful business owner at 33 years old was nothing to downplay. Most people would be proud of themselves, and Jai was… mostly. But every time she felt that sense of pride, there was that little nagging feeling that she was only succeeding because she was neglecting her personal relationships. And hadn't that been one of Elliot's chief complaints? That she was too busy, and when she *was* around, she was cold. Or too clingy. He couldn't seem to decide how he wanted her to be.

And there it was again. How *he* wanted her to be. And like a fool, Jai had done her best to conform to that, while still in the throes of bringing Honeybee to fruition. Elliot hated that. Looking back with a clear mind, Jai could see just how hateful and manipulative he had been. One minute he would be insulting her cooking, telling her that the decor was tacky, or citing the terrifying statistics on how often new restaurants failed. The next, he would be trying, and failing, to get her into bed. It was a crazy, dysfunctional cycle.

But the man was gone, and Honeybee was still here. Critics raved about her cooking, a local design magazine had chosen the restaurants cream, gold, and black-accented interior for the cover of their biggest issue of the year, and Honeybee *hadn't* failed. Jai hadn't failed.

"You're right," she said to Cameron, pulling herself away from her thoughts.

Cameron smiled. "*Duh.* Jai, success comes naturally to you, but I don't think you see it. You've got that perfect body that you don't have to work for, gorgeous skin, gorgeous hair. You can cook like nobody's business, and look at what you've built, from *nothing* with Honeybee. You got all the good traits; nothing was left over for me!"

Even though Cameron was laughing, Jai detected a pain behind her words that she'd never noticed before. "Cam… why do you say that?"

"Jai, I have to put a lot of planning into everything if I want it to go well. You can just go with the flow and make things work. I *wish* I could get away with that."

There was no bitterness in Cameron's words; she was simply making an observation. Still, Jai felt bad for her sister. Is that why things had spiraled so far out of control for her? Because the break-up with Kyle, then the subsequent accident, had put her off plan?

"Anyway, back to the point," Cameron said, fiddling with one of her earrings, "I think we should have Rashad do some pictures for the story as well. He can do the shoot right here in the restaurant."

"Pictures of *me*?"

"Yeah…"

Jai shook her head. "Uh-uh. I don't know about that."

"That's ok. I do," Cameron said, smiling as she gathered her things. "I have to get back over to the office, but we'll set up some time to do your interview, and the photo shoot. You can even talk to Rashad yourself about artistic direction."

"It doesn't sound like I have a choice."

"Good. Cause you don't. It'll be great!"

"Mmhmm." Jai grinned, following Cameron to the front door. They exchanged hugs, and then Cameron was on her way.

Halfway through the door into the kitchen, Jai turned, distracted by the sound of her name. She was surprised to see Leslie, Brian's fiancé, walking toward her, with no trace of her usual smile on her face.

"Leslie, hi! Can I help you with something, or are you here to eat? Lunch service is over, but—"

"I'm not here for that," Leslie said, fidgeting with the purse strap on her shoulder.

"Oh… Well, Brian isn't here today."

"I know, that's why I came. I wanted to talk to you."

Jai's eyes widened. "Me? Oh… ok. Do you want to come into my office?"

Leslie nodded, and Jai motioned for her to follow as she led the way to her office. She left the door open, in case Leslie was planning something crazy. Jai took a swig from the bottle of water on her desk as she sat down on the couch, with Leslie beside her.

"Um… I'll just get straight to the point, I guess. Are you sleeping with Brian?"

Jai choked, covering her mouth to contain her coughs. "Am I— what? No! *No!* Why would you even think that?"

Leslie's eyes were sad as she replied. "I'm just trying to figure out what's going on. Since we moved in together, Brian has been picking fights, staying out really late, supposedly working a bunch of extra hours. He's just been really moody or something lately and I don't know why."

So there were three things wrong with that. First, Brian hadn't mentioned a single clue that he and Leslie were *living together*. Secondly, she didn't know where Brian had been spending his late nights, but it certainly wasn't at Honeybee. They had just hired a second assistant manager, so if anything, his work load was less. Third, every time he was around Jai, Brian had been in a great mood, and his usual, overly flirty self.

"Wow… I don't know what to say, Leslie. But I can assure that I'm *not* sleeping with your fiancé, and I never have."

Leslie squirmed, as if she were uncomfortable with the conversation.

Join the club.

"Jai, I don't know how to say this without coming off the wrong way, but… I'm not sure if I believe you."

Jerking her head back, Jai felt her heartbeat start racing as Leslie continued. "I mean, Brian is a handsome guy, you're a pretty, single girl. I know you guys have been friends for a long time, so it's not exactly a stretch that something would happen between you two."

"But I'm not single." Jai's face grew hot at the 'humph" Leslie muttered under her breath, with a derisive smirk that clearly implied disbelief. "*Not* that I have to share anything with you, but I've been dating someone for the last five months. I'm not thinking about Brian like that, so maybe you should be sitting *him* down to talk about this."

'Since you want to get an attitude, bitch' is how Jai wanted to end that last statement, but she forced herself to calm down. After all, the unspoken truth was that eight months ago, she *was* thinking about Brian like that, and she'd been knocked back into her lane.

But, it wasn't like Jai had ill intent. She had fully expected her affection to be reciprocated, and as far as she knew, Brian hadn't even been serious about Leslie at the time. Now, it seemed like he was doing a careful job of cultivating exactly how Jai saw his relationship with Leslie. But why? He was about to marry the girl, and Jai had moved on to Derek. Whatever his reasons were, he was also being less than truthful with his future wife, which ultimately wasn't Jai's problem.

"I've tried," Leslie explained as her shoulders sank. "He just brushes it off, like I'm being silly." She had dropped the attitude, but Jai's sympathy had declined. At this point, she was just annoyed that not only had Brian disappointed her, he had pulled her into drama with his fiancé.

"Again, Leslie. I don't know what you want me to say."

"Nothing, I guess. You denied that you're sleeping with him, so I guess that's it." Leslie stood, and Jai followed, eager to see her out

130

of the office. "But for the record, I'm not convinced. He told me that you kissed him."

Jai started to speak, then hesitated, considering her words before she continued. "That's true, and it was wrong of me. I was mistaken about the nature of your relationship when it happened, but it still wasn't okay. I won't deny that. But that's the most... uh, intimate— that Brian and I have ever been. I have a man, who I love. Your man is just that: *yours.*"

"Brian hasn't mentioned a single thing about you dating someone."

"It seems to me like Brian isn't mentioning a lot."

Leslie rolled her eyes. "Look, you don't have to lie—"

"Jai?" They both looked to the open door to see Derek standing there, handsome as ever in a crisp white polo and khakis.

"Baby! Hey!" Jai tried not to appear smug as she greeted Derek with a kiss, looping her arm around his waist as she turned back to Leslie, whose eyes were wide as she stared up at Derek.

"Derek, this is Brian's fiancé, Leslie. Leslie, this is my Derek."

A flush crept across Leslie's almond colored skin. "Oh. Well... nice to meet you. I'll see you later Jai."

I hope not.

"Ok, you take care." Jai closed the door behind Leslie's retreating back, then turned to give Derek another kiss, but he held up a hand, stopping her.

"Wait just a minute," he said, frowning. "Why was she in here grilling you about Brian? Is there something I need to know?"

Throwing her hands up in the air, Jai paced across the office. "What is this, 'pick on Jai' day? Damn. No. Just like I told her, there's nothing to know about me and Brian!"

"Wow... o-kay."

Jai let out a heavy sigh as she turned back to him. "I'm sorry for snapping at you babe, I just feel a little beat down. First Cameron was here getting on to me, then Leslie accusing me of sleeping with Brian, and now you."

Derek's expression immediately softened and he extended his arms to her. "I didn't mean to gang up on you babe," he said, pulling her into a hug. "*I'm* sorry."

"No, you have a right to want to know, but I assure you, Brian and I are just friends. You remember what you told me when I got mad at you about Jessica? That I was the only person on your mind? Well, the same applies here. Yeah, I thought there was something there with Brian, and I pursued it. But that was before I even knew you. And since then, it's only been you. I really like you, Derek."

He bent to place a kiss on her lips before he spoke. "That's not what you told ol' girl."

"What?"

"You told her that you *loved* me."

"I said that? I don't think I—"

"Hush," he said, before dipping his head again to give her a kiss that made her toes curl. "I love you too."

— & —
Cameron
Sunday, January 25th

"Come to your door."

What?

Cameron pulled the phone away from her ear, looking at the time displayed in the top corner of her screen.

"Will, why the hell are you calling me at nine in the morning on a Sunday?"

"Simmer down, and come open the door."

Groaning, she flipped the covers back and sat up, taking a moment to stretch. She briefly considered leaving him standing outside, since he showed up unannounced, but she was starting to get used to it. Since the night he had taken her to his daughter's basketball game, he had popped up 2 other times. Both had been early morning visits to her office, after finishing an overnight shift in the ambulance. Both times, he came bearing donuts.

Cameron wanted one of those donuts.

A glance in the mirror satisfied her concern that the tee shirt and shorts she slept in covered a sufficient amount of skin, but after a short deliberation, she did decide to do a quick rinse of mouthwash. No reason to *completely* gross the man out.

By the time she made it to the door, Will was calling again, probably wondering what was taking her so long. Cameron grinned as she hit the 'decline' button on the call, then flung the door open, pasting a look of mock-annoyance on her face.

The annoyance melted away at the sight of the huge bouquet of roses Will held out to her. She accepted them, then moved to the side to let him in.

"Oh my goodness, what are these for?"

Will placed the bags he carried, which smelled like sausage and waffles, on the counter before he spoke. "Hold out your hand and close your eyes."

"For what?"

"What's with all the questions?

Cameron laughed. "What's with all the demands?"

"Just roll with it, damn."

Placing one hand on her hip, Cameron held out the other, with her palm up, then closed her eyes. Her skin tingled in response to his touch as he grabbed her hand, closing it over a small cold object. Will kept his hand covering hers, but instructed her to open her eyes.

"You ready?"

Cameron squirmed, bouncing on the balls of her feet. "Of course I'm ready, let me see!"

Chuckling, he released her hand. She opened it and gasped. "Is this?"

"Yep," he said, clapping his hand on her shoulder. "It is."

Tears sprang to Cameron's eyes as she stared down at the large metal token in her hand, engraved with '1 month'. "How did you get this?"

"I talked to Jai, and she talked your therapist into giving it to her so you wouldn't have to wait until tomorrow for it. I mean, your one month sober mark is *today*. You shouldn't have to wait just because it's Sunday."

Will didn't even budge when Cameron launched herself at him, wrapping her arms around his waist in a fierce hug. She willed herself not to cry, but when he returned her embrace, she broke down, sobbing into his chest until her throat was sore.

"Hey." Will stepped back, using one finger to tip up her chin. "Jai would be here, but—"

"She thought you should be the one to give it to me, since you made me start seeing the therapist."

"Something like that."

Sniffling, Cameron nodded, remembering the conversation she'd had with her sister the week before. Jai had been skeptical of her insistence that her relationship with Will was platonic, but it was the truth. Cameron didn't need a man. She needed healing, and friendship. So far, he was providing both, and even in such a short time, she valued him a lot.

"We're proud of you, Cam."

She looked up, her eyes brimming with tears again as they met his. For a short moment, she had the urge to raise herself on her bare toes, lifting her mouth in the universal invitation for a kiss. They were still in each other's arms, and Cameron found herself suddenly very aware of the warm, spicy scent of his cologne and the powerful hardness of his body against hers.

"Thank you." She stepped away from his embrace, looking around for a distraction. "These are gorgeous," she said, when her eyes landed on the vibrant peach-colored roses.

Will cleared his throat. "Uh, yeah. One for every day of your sobriety."

"Really? This was really thoughtful, Will. I had no idea you had it in you to do something like this. Jai must have told you what to do?"

"No, actually. I decided on my own. I decided on this on my own too." He opened the bag that smelled like food, and Cameron's mouth watered as the scent grew stronger. She let out of a soft sigh, watching with a grin on her face as he place a plate loaded with breakfast in front of her. Then, he pulled out a final package, holding it up so that she could see the logo on the bag.

"Donuts!"

— & —
Jai
Tuesday, February 10th

This wasn't a good idea. This is a bad, bad, bad, idea.

Jai stared at herself in the mirror again, wondering how she had allowed Rashad to talk her into wearing lingerie for this photo shoot for Sugar & Spice. Well, it hadn't *only* been him. Cameron thought it was a 'fun' idea as well, so Jai was preparing herself go back out into the now-empty kitchen in nothing but the lacy white boy shorts and bra her sister had chosen. Oh, and a black chef's coat. She was going to be posing on a stainless steel counter in lingerie and a chef's coat.

This is a bad idea.

A knock on the office door startled her, causing her to stumble on the hot pink stilettos she wore.

Bad idea.

She pulled on her robe, belting it tightly at her waist before opening the door to Brian's smiling face.

It hadn't even been two weeks since the uncomfortable conversation with Leslie, and Jai was still annoyed about it. Brian had basically denied any responsibility, excusing himself by implying that Leslie was just overreacting, and embellishing the extent of his bad behavior because she was upset. Jai could tell a cop-out when she saw one, but she reminded herself that it really wasn't her business anyway. If he wanted to act like there wasn't a problem, fine, there wasn't.

"I've got something to tell you," he walked past her without waiting for a response, turning to face her once he was well inside the office.

"Um... ok?" She frowned, confused, when he grabbed her hand to pull her close.

"I ended it with Leslie. We're in the clear, babe."

Jai snatched her hand away from Brian, then pushed him away. "What the hell do you mean 'we're in the clear'? What are you talking about?"

Brian smiled again, even bigger this time, and Jai had to silently talk herself down from smacking the grin from his face. "I'm talking about you and me, sweetheart. It was stupid of me to propose to Leslie, knowing how you felt. But I fixed it now! We can finally b—"

"Whoa. Whoa, whoa, *whoa.* Slow your roll, Brian." Jai closed her eyes for a moment, trying to gather her composure. "You're saying that you broke off your engagement with Leslie... for *me*?"

"That's exactly what I'm saying baby. We—"

"No no no. No. I'm not available to you." Jai shook her head, placing her hands on her hips as she paced the room. "Are you crazy? Did you completely forget about Derek? The man I've been dating for almost five months?"

"It's sweet that you're worried about his feelings, but—"

"I'm sorry, worried about his feelings? Why would I be worried about his feelings?" Jai's question was met with a blank look, and she quickly realized where the confusion was. "Wait a second...

you think that I'm gonna break up with Derek?"

Brian shrugged. "Why wouldn't you?"

"Why wou—" Jai stopped pacing long enough to laugh at just how ridiculous this entire situation was. "Brian... I'm *not* breaking up with him. He's a wonderful guy, he's incredibly good to me, and I love him."

"Come on, Jai," Brian said, scoffing at her words. "I know you told Leslie that bullshit, but we both know the real deal."

Jai threw her hands up. "No, I need you to tell me. Please explain what you think is happening here."

"I think we've been friends for ten years. I think we have feelings for each other that are no longer just friendly, so I think we should explore it."

"And you realize this *now*? Instead of last year, when I bared my heart to you, now that I've moved on and have someone who loves me back, *now* you want explore it."

Brian grabbed her hand, attempting to pull her into his arms. "That was different, Jai."

"It wasn't!" she smacked his hands away. "It's not any different. It was wrong of me then, and it's wrong of you now. It's selfish, Brian. We can't just screw up two other people's lives to explore what could have been. They don't deserve that."

"Could have been?"

Jai nodded. "Yes, could have been." She crossed her arms over her chest. "Brian, I don't feel the same I felt way the night I decided to take a chance and kiss you."

"What changed?"

"*I* changed. And... my view of you has changed. I offered my heart to you, and you refused it. Derek didn't."

Brian cocked his head to the side. "So that's where we stand?"

"Yeah. You should probably see if you fiancé will take you back."

"I don't want her back. I want you."

Jai walked over to the door and pulled it open. "I've gotta finish getting ready for this photo shoot, Brian. You should go."

"We aren't done talking about this, Jai."

"Actually, Brian, yes. We are."

— & —

Rashad
Late Tuesday Night

"This isn't working."

Jai rolled her eyes and sat up, closing her coat over the rather delicious view of her caramel skin in the white lingerie. If she was there, Rashad would have thanked Cameron for what he considered to be a personal gift to him: Jai's fine ass in that angelic white lace and those hot pink heels that made her legs seem even longer. She had a flat stomach, but the rest of her body consisted of lush curves, begging to be touched.

But, Rashad valued his life. Derek was shooting death glares at anyone whose eyes rested below Jai's neck any longer than a few seconds, and Rashad had no interest in finding out what would happen if Derek decided to do more that just scowl.

More importantly though, it was obvious that Jai wasn't into the shoot. She looked incredible, but her body language was stiff, and smiling or not, she really didn't look like she wanted to be there. There was no way these pictures would make it into Sugar & Spice. Not with Rashad's name on them.

"Jai, you wanna tell me what's going on?" Rashad approached her carefully, keeping one eye on her, the other on Derek.

"Can we just get this over with? I'm cold, and I'm starting to get stiff, and I—"

"I see where this is going. Why don't you take a break while do some lighting adjustments? Maybe that will help these shots not look so…"

"Bad?" Jai finished, crossing her arms. The move pushed her breasts even closer together and Rashad forced himself to look away.

"I wasn't gonna say that, but…"

"Kiss my ass, Rashad."

Grinning, he took another step closer, bending his head to speak quietly into her ear. He knew he was risking his safety with Derek standing just a few yards away, but he couldn't resist. "You know I'll do more than kiss it, right?"

"Ugh!" Rashad laughed as Jai shoved him away, clenching her chef's coat against her body as she slid down from the counter and stomped away. His smile slipped as Derek entered his line of sight, but instead of coming toward Rashad, he followed Jai down the hall to her office.

— &—

Jai

"Aah!" Jai clapped a hand over her mouth, quieting a squeal as Derek lifted her onto her desk. His hands trailed under her chef's coat, then over the lacy cups of her bra, causing a moan of appreciation to slip from her throat.

He kissed her, softly at first, then slipped his tongue into her mouth, kissing her with an energy that was almost frantic. "Do you have any idea how sexy you are? When I saw you up there on that counter—" he gently nipped her neck "— I've been waiting all night to do this." He grabbed the waistband of the tiny boy shorts with one hand, using the other the lift her so that he could slid them down over her hips. He flung them to the side, pulling her bottom lip into his mouth as he slid his fingers inside of her.

Jai relaxed her body against his, enjoying the friction as he stroked them in and out in a slow, sensual rhythm. "Mmm. Damn, I needed this," she whimpered into his shoulder.

"Tense?"

"You have no idea." She lifted her head, looking him in the eyes as she unbuckled his belt and unzipped his jeans, anxiously forcing them, along with his boxers, down his legs.

The incident with Brian had left her feeling stressed and annoyed. The last thing Jai felt like doing was vamping in front of a camera, when she really wanted to haul her *former* best friend back into her office and kick his ass. She had texted Derek to come to the shoot, hoping that seeing his face would put her in a better mood.

Even though it was late, and he had a patient early the next morning, he had agreed to come. There in her office, with Derek palming her backside in preparation to push himself inside of her, Jai felt very, very relaxed.

— & —

Rashad

Look at this lucky motherfucker.

Rashad chuckled to himself. Derek was standing off the side, with a silly grin on his face while one of the assistants touched up Jai's makeup. He still had traces of her hot pink lipstick on his neck and collar, and a small bruise had suddenly appeared just above the

138

waistband of Jai's panties. It looked suspiciously like a hickey. Rashad knew *exactly* what they had been doing.

But he wasn't mad. Jealous, maybe, but definitely not mad. Jai was visibly more relaxed, and when she climbed back onto the cold steel counter to take another round of photos, the difference was like night and day. She looked right at Derek as she posed, openly teasing and flirting with him. Somehow, Jai was able to make chopping spinach and peeling potatoes look like the sexiest thing in the world. He was definitely going to be sending a thank you card to Cameron.

Best assignment ever.

Chapter Ten
— & —
Jai
Wednesday, February 11th

"I'm sorry, *what?*"

Jai raised an eyebrow.

"I *said*, 'I guess you're the bitch he's trying to replace me with.'"

Did she just call me a bitch? In my *restaurant? Why do all the crazy people come* here *to be crazy?*

Taking a deep breath, Jai really looked at the woman standing in front of her. She had her hands on her hips, and her pretty face was twisted into a scowl. Jai had no idea who this woman was, but after the month of drama she had experienced between stupid ass Brian and Leslie, she certainly wasn't in the mood to handle more.

"So... you're not about clown in here, ma'am. I don't know what the problem is, or who you think I am, but you've got to get out of here." Jai spoke quietly, not wanting to call any more attention to the scene. It was the end of the lunch service at Honeybee, and the place as, as usual, crowded. Jai was only out of the kitchen because one of the waitresses had come to her in tears, saying that one of the customers was insisting on speaking to a manager. She was dealing with a flare-up that morning, so Brian was more useful in the kitchen than she was.

"Bit—"

"I'm not your bitch, ok?" Jai held up a warning finger and moved closer to the woman, causing her to flinch and take a step back.

"Fine, *Jai*. I'm not going anywhere until you promise to leave my man alone."

"What man?"

"Derek."

Jai's eyes narrowed and it clicked for her exactly who she was dealing with.

"You must be Jessica."

Jessica smirked, flipping her thick, wavy hair over her shoulder. "So you've heard about me. Good. Now back the fuck off."

"Why, exactly, would I do that?" Jai asked, cocking her head to the side. "Derek and I are close. *Very* close. I don't know where you got it into your head that he was your man, but you're dumb as hell if you're sticking around for whatever scraps are left after the time, energy, and attention he gives *me.*"

Jai had no reason to feel threatened. Like she had told Derek before, she knew exactly the kind of woman Jessica was, and the exactly the games she played. She had seen and dealt with it before, in the craziness of her early dating years. This woman was going to have to try harder if she wanted to 'scare' Jai.

Just as she suspected, Jessica's smirk faltered. "Look, Derek and I were a couple for three years. This isn't the first time we've broken up. We *always* get back together, but this time, you're standing in the way of that."

"That's not my problem, Jessica. Derek and I have been together for several months, and *our* relationship has progressed to a point that I know he's not thinking about you, so..."

Jessica sucked her teeth. "Duh, because you're distracting him... somehow."

"You know what? I'm done with this. You've gotta go." Jai turned toward the front of the restaurant, flagging down two of her waiters. "Get her out of here," she said when they approached. Not bothering to look back, she walked away.

Jai stumbled from the force of Jessica shoving her in the back. She saw red, and her fists clenched reflexively as she turned. Jessica was saying something, fighting against the waiters as they held her back, but Jai heard none of it. Her hand had traveled most of the necessary distance to connect with her face when someone caught her around the wrist.

"Brian, let me go!" She struggled to release herself from his grip, but he grabbed the other arm, pulling her closer.

"Jai, stop it. The customers!" he whispered fiercely, nodding his head toward the tables. She glanced in the direction he indicated, and sure enough, the last of the remaining customers from lunch were staring at the scene, whispering among themselves.

Common sense took over, and she stopped fighting against him. "Get that bitch out of here before I kill her."

"Ok, I got it, but you need to cool off. Go wait in your office, I'll handle it."

Jai shot Jessica one last look before she stalked away. She slammed the door closed when she reached her office, but didn't sit down. Her office had been specifically designed as a peaceful place; somewhere she could go after a hectic service and escape from the noise and stress. Now, it only reminded her of the drama with Leslie and Brian.

What the hell was happening around here? Honeybee meant everything to her, yet people were choosing *this* as the apparent battleground for whatever misguided grievances they had against her. She was sick of it. She made a mental note to hire a security guard. There was no way she was dealing with this nonsense again. The next person that decided to confront her was getting their ass kicked, one way or another.

"Jai, what the hell was that?" Brian blazed through the door, pulling off his coat. "In front of a packed house, you were gonna fight that girl?"

A new flush of heat rushed through her body as she snapped back. "She put her damn hands on me Brian. I was walking away until she did *that*!"

"Oh please, Jai. Don't forget that I've known you since we were teenagers. What were you gonna do, kick her ass and take her man like you did that girl in college?"

Jai drew in a breath. "How dare you?" she asked, keeping her tone low and controlled.

"Oh, don't try to act all high and mighty. You did it back then, you were ready to do it to Leslie, and now you're doing it to Jessica, running around here with Derek. Did you steal Elliot from somebody too?"

Jai didn't think twice about smacking Brian in the face. She actually enjoyed the sting it left behind on her hand. "You are such a piece of shit. You *know* that's not who I am, and I can't believe you're trying to turn it on me, like I'm some whore running seducing people!"

"You tried to seduce me, Jai!" he said, throwing his hands up into the air. "You can hit me because you're mad all you want to, but the fact is, you never have wanted a man that you didn't have to take from someone else. Look at us! When I was with Leslie, you were ready to be all over me, but once I break up with her for you, all of a sudden you're in love with this Derek dude."

"Are you kidding me?! Brian, you were the one who was constantly flirting, and touching, and making me think there was something there when there wasn't. We were best friends! I had feelings for you, and *you told me that it wasn't serious with Leslie*," she accused, jabbing a finger in his face as she spoke. "So yeah, I went for it. The girl from college that you're throwing in my face was just as delusional as this Jessica chick is. The only difference is that her boyfriend was playing both of us. Elliott was single, and so was Derek. Even his crazy ass ex admits that, she's just mad because she wants to get back with him. So fuck you, Brian. How dare you try to make me seem like something I'm not?"

Her hands were shaking when she turned away from him, yanking the ponytail holder from her wrists to pull her locs away from her face. When Brian didn't respond, she turned back to see him staring down at his feet, with his hands shoved into his pockets. She lost a bit of her steam when he looked up, a pained expression in his eyes when they met hers.

"I'm sorry, Jai."

His words hung in the air for a moment before he continued. "I wasn't trying to attack you."

"Well it really fucking sounded like it."

"I know. It's just... listen, I—"

"I really don't care to hear what you have to say, Brian." For the first time, Jai felt the moisture running down her cheeks, and reached up to wipe her face. She waved Brian off when he tried to approach her.

"Jai, please. I need you to hear this."

She scoffed, shaking her head. "I can't believe you think I care about what you need right now. You came in here and accused me of being a home wrecker, and a whore. Fuck what you need! That girl came into *my* restaurant and purposely started an altercation with me, but you're on her side. So why don't you go talk to her?"

"I *did* talk to her, Jai, and she told me that Derek has always had a problem being faithful. She says that they're still sleeping together."

"You are so stupid." Jai laughed as she sat down on the edge of the desk. "If he's such a damn dog, why does she want him? *She's lying.* I'm sure she thought she would just feed the bullshit to you, you would pass it to me, and I would be dumb enough to believe it. I don't trust a single word out of her mouth."

"What if she's telling the tru—?"

"She's not!" Jai closed her eyes, blowing out a heavy breath. "She's. Not. That bitch is lying through her teeth, and I'm tired of talking about it, ok? And quite frankly I'm tired of arguing with you. I'm tired of *looking* at you. Just get out."

"Jai, wh—"

"Out!"

Brian shook his head as he stomped toward the door and yanked it open. "Don't come crying to me when you find out that motherfucker is lying to you."

He slammed the door behind him before Jai could respond, and she forced herself to stay seated instead of following to curse him out again. How had their relationship gotten this far off course? She couldn't even be sure if he were looking out for her best interests or just trying to exploit an opening. She was, however, sure that Jessica was a liar.

That bitch was *definitely* lying.

— & —

Cameron
February 20th - Friday Morning

I'm such a liar. I should have let the interns do this.

Cameron looked around at the room full of people, wishing that she had delegated this task to someone else. She had never been good at handling crowds, and this event was exception. But, this was necessary. Sugar & Spice had been invited to the yearly career fair before Cameron's accident and she had accepted the invitation, so there was no way she backing out.

But this *crowd.* Man, the crowd had her stress levels through the roof, and Cameron really, really, really wanted a drink. Just something small, like a glass of wine. Moscato, even. Yes, a glass of moscato would be amazing to take her mind off of this crowd. And the fact that she was still painfully single. Yes, one simple little glass of moscato, which was barely wine. More like juice. It would be so perfect!

"Ms. Taylor!"

Cameron rolled her eyes at the sound of her name. She picked up one of the information packets she'd brought with her from the office and tried not to look bored as she turned to give the same ten minute spiel about entrepreneurship and journalism she'd been giving all morning.

"Oh, Kelly!" Cameron smiled at the teenager as she stood up from the stool to give her a hug. Kelly had inherited her Will's smooth mahogany complexion, but her thick curly hair, dimples, and button nose were reminiscent of the honey-colored woman beside her.

"Mom, this Cameron Taylor, the *owner* of Sugar & Spice magazine. Ms. Taylor, this is my mom, Stephanie."

Stephanie extended her hand, sending a warm smile to Cameron. "I'm a big fan of the magazine. Especially this last issue, with all those delicious half-naked people."

"You must be referring to the 'Life Savers' issue," Cameron laughed.

"Mmhm. I bought two!" She waved two fingers in the air for emphasis as she giggled with Kelly.

"Well thank you. I appreciate the support, and I know the charities will as well."

"You're very welcome. I thought your story was really amazing. That was crazy, that Will was the one who pulled you out of the car!"

For some reason, Cameron felt a strange sensation flood her body at Stephanie's mention of Will. But why? Obviously they had a child together, so of course they spoke to each other. Cameron knew they weren't married, and never had been, but that didn't mean they weren't still dating or sleeping together. They didn't exactly avoid the subject when they talked, but Will never brought it up, so Cameron didn't either, not wanting to give the impression that it mattered. Because it didn't.

"Yeah," Cameron said, forcing more enthusiasm than she felt. "It was kind of surreal to just randomly meet him like that, but it was cool, at the same time."

"I bet. He told me that you guys have become friends."

"Oh. Uh, yeah, we have. He uh, helped me get the support I

needed to deal with the accident." She kept her tone light, so it wouldn't betray the shakiness of her voice. Just how much had Will shared with Stephanie about her situation?

"Yeah, he's a little... um, abrupt, but he's good about being there for his friends."

"Uh, yeah. So, Kelly! What brings you to the career fair? From what I saw out there on the court I assumed you would be sticking with sports for your career path."

Kelly smiled. "I really don't even like basketball that much. I just play because I'm grateful that I actually can, after everything that happened with my accident."

"Hey, I like how you think! That's pretty cool," Cameron said. "So what is that you *really* want to do?"

"I would love to be a journalist, and maybe even own a magazine one day, like you."

"Oh, in that case I *love* how you think," Cameron laughed. "I may have to look into a summer internship for you, if that's ok with your parents."

Excited, Kelly turned to her mother, who nodded her approval.

"O-M-G, thank you so much!" Cameron smiled as the teenager pulled her into a hug. "Ms. Taylor, are you doing anything tonight?" Kelly asked, still wearing a bright smile.

Confused, Cameron looked between mother and daughter.

"Please forgive my daughter. I think she's trying to invite you come out with us to the movies, but I'm sure you probably already have plans," Stephanie said, giving Kelly a 'look'. Cameron quickly bit the inside of her cheek, hoping to distract herself from the sudden tightness in her throat. Of course she didn't have plans, she was alone. While Jai was hugged up with Derek, Cameron would be spending her Friday night trying not to drown herself in the bottom of bottle.

"Dad said she was single though!"

Cameron's shoulders slumped as her ears and necked turned hot. "Uh, Kelly is right, but I couldn't possibly intrude on your family thing."

"Of course you can," Stephanie said, grabbing Cameron's hand. "You're Will's friend, so you're welcome to tag along."

Cameron cocked an eyebrow. "It's a thing with Will?"

Kelly nodded. "Yeah. Dad takes us out a few weekends every month. We always have an amazing time!"

"He says he likes to make sure his favorite girls know what a good date is like. And the way he talks about you, 'Cameron said this, Cameron did that', I'm sure you qualify."

So... he talks to her about me?

"I don't know about this." Cameron shook her head. "If Will wanted me to come along, he would have invited me."

"He probably just doesn't wanna be weird," Kelly said. "You know, asking you out on a date and all?"

"I guess I could see that. But, still—"

"Still nothing," Stephanie interrupted. You're coming, and that's that. Will knows where to find you. We'll see you at seven!"

And then they were gone. Kelly tossed a wave and a smile over her shoulder as they walked away, leaving Cameron confused. Had she just been roped into some kind of weird, cult-orgy thing? Was Will still sleeping with Stephanie? Was this Stephanie's way of scoping out the competition? There were way too many questions, with not enough answers.

As baffled as she was about her sudden plans, this little encounter had been the sign she needed to get any romantic notions about Will off of her mind. Even though Cameron knew Stephanie had to be in her thirties, she barely looked any older than Kelly, and she was ridiculously pretty. If things ever did go past friendship with Will, she would never feel comfortable with Stephanie around. Not after the debacle with Angie and Kyle. Nope. She wasn't going to ever deal with something like that again.

There would never be a 'Will and Cameron'. *Ever.*

— & —
Will
Friday Night

"How long do you think it will take Kelly and Stephanie to start up a 'Will and Cameron forever' campaign?" Will grinned over at Cameron, who was seated beside him on the bench. She didn't look away from whatever had her attention, so he followed her gaze directly to the bar.

Shit.

Will had tried to steer his daughter away from that particular arcade after they left the movie, knowing that it was one of those combo things that served alcohol right across from skee-ball machines. But Kelly had insisted, so Stephanie had insisted, so *Cameron* had insisted, not knowing the temptation that the arcade held. He didn't have a chance to warn her before the three women had taken off across the street, hand in hand like teenagers.

He really, really wished he had tried harder. She had that look in her eyes again, that glassy, haunted look that she'd worn at Christmas. One he thought he'd never see again.

"Hey," he placed a hand over hers, and his touch seemed to get her attention. She flinched, then turned to face him, blinking rapidly like she had just woken up.

"Hey! I'm sorry, what did you say?"

"Nothing important." He leaned closer, speaking into her ear so he wouldn't have to yell over the chaotic din of laughter and the game machines. "Are you ok?"

She blinked again, then looked back to the bar. "I— no. No, I'm not."

A few minutes later, they were in Will's truck, heading to Cameron's apartment. He'd told Stephanie that Cameron wasn't feeling well, and she insisted that he take her home, while she and Kelly stayed. The wink that Stephanie had given him, along with instructions to 'take good care of Cameron' gave him a little pause. He wanted to ask where the innuendo was coming from, but that conversation would have to wait until later.

"You cold?" he asked, noticing that she had her arms clutched around herself. He reached for the heat settings on the dashboard, but she grabbed his hand, pulling it back.

"No. It's fine."

She didn't release his hand for a few more minutes, but Will didn't mention it. He kept his eyes focused on the road as they turned into the parking deck for her building. He couldn't speak for Cameron, but he was getting very good at ignoring the increasingly frequent sparks between them. There was no way Will was going to be the one to make things awkward. From what he saw tonight, Cameron was still struggling with her addiction, and he wanted to kick his own ass for contributing to it.

They sat there in silence for a full minute after he cut the ignition, listening to the sounds of the traffic from the nearby street.

"I'm sorry, Cam." He reached over the center console to place a hand on her knee. "This is my fault. I should have—"

"Will, shut up. This isn't your fault; it was just one of those days." She unbuckled herself then turned sideways, pulling her feet up into the seat. "Not a *bad* day, just… hard. It happens sometimes." She rested her cheek against the headrest. It was nearly eleven at night, and her eyelids hung heavily over her eyes. Cameron still looked sad, but not quite as haunted.

The sudden desire to pull her into an embrace tugged at Will, but he kept his back planted firmly against his own seat, watching her.

"What?" she asked, picking at her nails. "You look like you have something to say. What's on your mind?"

Will shook his head. "Nothing."

"Nothing, or nothing you're gonna tell me?"

"Nothing I'm gonna tell you."

"That's fine." She shrugged. "So, on Tuesday I get my two month token."

Good girl.

"Are you throwing hints? You're expecting what, *sixty* roses this time?"

"What? No, I was just telling yo—"

"Yeah right. You're greedy, Cam." He tried to hold his serious expression, but after a few seconds, he broke into a smile.

She swatted his hand, but couldn't help a grin from taking over her face. "You make me sick."

"No I don't."

"You're right," she said, tilting her head to the side. "You don't, actually. You're a pretty good friend. I appreciate you, Will. You didn't have to leave your date with your family for me."

"Ah, shit. Don't get all Hallmark card on me, Cam."

Her nose wrinkled as she laughed.

Did it always do that?

"I'm not trying to be corny, I promise. I just… I wanted you to know that I appreciate you."

"Message received. Now are you gonna sit here in my truck all night?"

Cameron started to speak, but her words were taken over by a yawn. "Well," she said when she recovered. "I guess that's your answer. I need to go get my butt in the bed, and you need to get back to Stephanie before she comes after me."

"Was that your way of asking if anything was going on with me and Stephanie?"

"It sure was."

"Stephanie and I happened 16 years ago. We were college freshmen who got too drunk to think straight at a frat party, and she ended up pregnant. We only knew each other because we had a few classes together."

"And you guys really never…?"

"Other than that one time? *No.* She and I just never clicked like that, but we had a child to raise so we became friends. That's it, and that's all it will ever be. I'm not even Steph's type."

Cameron grinned. "Will, please. How could you not be her type? Does she like white boys or something?"

"No," Will chuckled. "Let's just say *you're* more Stephanie's type than I am."

"Oh. Ohh."

"Yeah. So, do you want me to walk you up?" They both knew that his asking was only a formality, but she nodded anyway, and turned to wait for him to open the car door. In front of her apartment, he waited while she fished her keys from her purse and unlocked the door. Before she went inside, she turned to Will, wrapping her arms around his waist for a hug. Reflexively, he placed a hand on the small of her back, pulling her in closer. Her head barely reached the top of his chest, so he had to bend to place a kiss on her forehead.

"Goodnight Cam."

She looked up, and Will saw a flash of *something* in her eyes just before she took advantage of his bent form and kissed him at the corner of his mouth.

"Goodnight, Will."

He was still standing in the same spot when he heard the door close behind her, and the deadbolt click in place.

What… what was that?

Chapter Eleven
— & —
Derek
Monday, March 2nd

Derek's stomach rolled as he stared down at the piece of plastic that had been unceremoniously shoved into his hand. There was no way... this had to be a trick. That's all it was, just another one of her desperate, manipulative games. It *had* to be.

"So are you just gonna sit there looking stupid, or are you gonna say something, *daddy*?" Jessica tossed her hair back as the satisfied smirk on her face became a full grin, further grating on Derek's already frayed nerves. She was enjoying this, and he wasn't surprised.

He should have known when Jessica called his line at the hospital, begging him to meet at her apartment that she was pulling out the big guns. This was her end-game, and probably had been all along. A pregnancy. How could he have been so stupid? His throat ached as he thought about Jai, and her possible reaction. It wouldn't be good. He knew exactly how she felt about the whole 'outside' baby situation with Cameron and Kyle, and he had no doubt that she would view this the same way. Technically, he *hadn't* cheated on her. They were broken up. As a matter of fact, the decision to become exclusive happened just a few hours after he slept with Jessica that one last time. Ok, so maybe she wouldn't hate him, but that didn't mean she would still want to be with him. Especially with a 'baby-mama' like Jessica.

"How far along are you?" he asked, narrowing his eyes at the mostly still-flat belly she was proudly displaying in a sweater cropped well above her midriff. He didn't bother to ask if she was going to have the baby. *Of course* she was going to, if it would keep him tied to her.

She shrugged. "However long ago you pinned me up against your front door and fucked me Derek, I don't know."

"You don't know?" Derek cocked his head to the side, lifting an eyebrow. "You really expect me to believe that?"

"Fine. A little over four months."

"Four months and not showing yet?"

Jessica sucked her teeth. "Duh. I'm *fit*. It takes a little longer."

"I don't believe you." He shook his head as he tossed the positive pregnancy test onto the table in front of him. "I think you're full of shit, and this is just another one of your little ploys to get me to break up with Jai, and get back with you."

"Believe whatever you want. Just know that in a month or two, I *will* be showing, and I'm gonna pay your little girlfriend a visit. I bet *she'll* believe it."

Derek's jaw clenched. "I told you to stay your ass away from Jai."

"Why?" she asked, laughing. "Do you think she's gonna be mad? Oh yeah, that's right… you were already dating her, and still sleeping with me."

"It was one time."

Jessica's hand rested on her belly. "And just that was enough, wasn't it? You'd better get going though," she said, walking to her front door. "I'm sure you need time to figure out what you're gonna do."

"What I'm gonna do?"

"Don't play dumb, Derek. You're a good guy. I know you're not gonna let me raise this baby by myself. We should be a family."

He wrinkled his brow. "You would just love that wouldn't you? I break up with Jai, and fall right in line with whatever ridiculous fantasy you have for your life?"

"Basically." She grinned as she opened the door with a flourish. "Like I said… you'll do the right thing."

— & —

Wednesday, March 18th

He had put it off long enough. Derek had to tell Jai about the baby, but once he did, he knew that would be the end of their relationship. He was already mourning the loss, but doing the best he could not to let it filter over to Jai. She was going through a mourning period of her own.

Jai had finally told him *everything* about the situation with Brian, and even though he wanted to be upset that she had hidden it from him, he kept it to himself. After all, it wasn't like he'd been completely forthcoming.

"What are you thinking about, handsome?" Jai approached him from behind, bending to drape her arms over his shoulders as he relaxed on the couch. He leaned back, using the soft cushion of her breasts to support his head as he looked up at her.

"Come sit down," he said. "I need to talk to you about something."

"Uh-oh." She gently removed her hands from his chest, then climbed over the back of the couch instead of walking around. Derek caught her just as she nearly rolled off the edge, pulling her into his lap. "That was close," she said, laughing. "But you rescued me." She planted a kiss softly against his lips. "My hero."

Damn, she is making this so hard.

"Derek, what's wrong?" She glided her hand over his hair, taking care not to disrupt his pattern of waves with her fingers. "You look so serious."

He sighed, unable to meet her eyes when he spoke. "Jessica is pregnant."

The hand stopped. "Oh. Okay. How far along is she?"

"Four months."

"Oh." Jai thought about that for a moment, then slowly extricated herself from his arms and stood, wrapping herself in her arms as she walked across the room.

"Jai, I—"

"Six months ago, Derek. That's when we started dating. So, if she's only four months pregnant…."

"Please give me a chance to explain."

"Explain *what*, Derek?" Her voice cracked, making Derek feel sick to his stomach.

He stood, crossing the room to reach her, but she jerked away, biting her bottom lip.

"It was before we decided we were going to be exclusive. You said that all that shit about me not being your man, and I was pissed off. Jessica stopped by, and—"

"So this is my fault?"

"*No.* I'm not saying that, I'm just trying to explain." He grabbed her hand, only to have it snatched away.

"Don't touch me! You know that was only about you not

telling me who I could be friends with, not giving you a pass to go screw around. And without a condom, Derek?"

"I used a condom, Jai. And you and I weren't sleeping together yet."

She jerked her head in his direction. "You think that makes it ok?"

"That's not what I said!"

"You may as well! 'We weren't exclusive yet, we weren't screwing, I used a condom, and you said I wasn't your man'. All of these excuses to make it seem like you weren't wrong!"

"But it's all the truth!"

Shit.

That was definitely the wrong thing to say.

"You're right," she said quietly, focusing her gaze on her bare toes.

"Jai..."

"No, Derek. You're right." She looked up, displaying eyes that were brimming with tears. "You were technically still single, and perfectly within your rights to sleep with whomever you wanted to. I gave you that freedom. So, you're right. I didn't want you questioning my friendship with Brian, so I did something stupid, and you took full advantage of it. I can't be mad about that."

Derek rubbed the back of his neck, feeling weak with relief. "Baby, I am *so* sorry. I promise you, I would never, ever cheat on you. You don't have to worry about that."

"Oh, I know." Her voice was strangely calm. "I said I couldn't be mad. That's not the same as being ok with it. Derek, I called you just a few hours later. I *told* you I had made a mistake, that I wanted us to be together."

"It happened before that though, Jai."

"Right, meaning you didn't even wait a full day before you screwed someone else!"

"Jai, —"

She shook her head. "No. Just go, Derek."

Derek swallowed past the dry, heavy lump in his throat. He tried to meet Jai's eyes, but she wouldn't look up, even as he placed a last kiss on her forehead as he left.

He had no idea how to clean this up.

Jai dropped to the floor, towel in hand to wipe up the hot spaghetti sauce that was now covering Cameron's white cabinets and tile floor. She had gone to Cameron's apartment to have lunch, hoping that cooking and spending a little time with her sister would give her at least a few moments of peace. Jai hadn't even realized her hand wasn't gripping the handle of the pan until she heard the sharp crack of it hitting the tile.

"Jai... get up." Cameron crouched down beside her, trying to pull her up from the floor.

Jai shook her head. "No, it'll stain your cabinets."

"Leave it," Cameron insisted, taking the towel from her hand. "It'll be fine. I want you to get up. It's your wrists again, isn't it?"

Jai reluctantly nodded. Without the towel, she had no reason to remain on the floor, but Jai couldn't find the energy to pull herself up. Instead, she sat back, slumping her body against the cabinets. Sighing, Cameron sat down beside her, threading her fingers through Jai's to clasp her hand. Jai rested her head on Cameron's shoulder, trying her best to hold back the tears that were still threatening to break free.

"Do you want me to ask Will to kick his ass? I know Derek is his best friend, but if I asked, I think he would do it."

Jai almost smiled. Cameron had been trying hard to make her feel better, but it was a pointless effort. Making it better would require going back in time. There was so much that could have been done differently, going *all* the way back to the disaster known as Elliot.

"No," Jai said, shaking her head. "He doesn't deserve that."

"Well *that's* subjective." Cameron wrapped her arm around Jai's shoulder. "He broke your heart. When Kyle broke *my* heart, you choked his ass."

"That was different. You were engaged, you know? You and Kyle had been together for years, you were planning a wedding. Derek slept with his ex after I told him he wasn't my man. It's not the same thing."

Cameron sucked her teeth. "He should have known you didn't mean that."

This time, Jai did laugh, because she'd almost told Derek the same thing, but she knew that wasn't fair. She couldn't expect him to read her mind. He'd reacted to something she said in anger, and she wasn't willing to accept the consequences.

"How did we end up so screwed up, sis?" Jai lifted her head, looking to Cameron, who shook her head.

"Don't say stuff like that, Jai. We're just... I don't know... going through an adjustment period, I think. This time last year, we both thought we were with the guys we were gonna marry. Now, we're both single, even though I think you should give Derek a chance."

Jai rolled her eyes. "And purposely put myself in Jessica's crosshairs? No thanks. I could have gotten past him sleeping with her, since as far as he knew, he was free to do that. But now that a baby is in the picture? No way."

"Well you *know* I get that," Cameron said, pressing the back of her head into the cabinet. "It's like... you can't hate *the baby*, because it didn't ask to be here, but if it didn't exist, you would be able to get past the pain. But a child is a *constant* reminder that neither of us needs."

Jai nodded. "Exactly. I'm doing the right thing, aren't I, Cam?"

"I asked you to same question about Kyle, and you told me it was something that I had to answer for myself. You have to do the same thing, sis."

"Ughhh. What good are you?"

"Oh hush. Get up and come see what Rashad emailed me."

"The pictures from my shoot?!"

Cameron grinned. "Yep!"

Jai jumped up, then helped Cameron from the floor as well. "What about the mess though? I think it's gonna leave stains."

"I'll get it while you look at the pictures, ok? I know how to clean my own damn kitchen, there's not gonna be any stains."

— & —
Cameron
Saturday Night

"That is definitely a stain."

Cameron rolled her eyes at the faint pink stains scattered across her lower cabinets and tile. Grumbling to herself about the choice of finishes in the overpriced apartment, she unlocked her Smartphone to do a web search for "removing stains from white cabinets".

Searching for cleaning tips at —she glanced at the clock— *two in the morning. What an exciting Saturday night, Cam. Way to go.*

She had been keeping Jai company, but she had dragged herself into the guest bedroom to sleep more than an hour ago, leaving Cameron alone to obsess about the cabinets. It was better than obsessing about her *real* problem, which nothing in the drawer beside her bed had been able to fix.

Finally, Cameron came across instructions that used ingredients she had on hand, so she began gathering the things on the list. She had just finished preparing her solution when a knock sounded at the door.

Cameron frowned. Who on earth would be showing up to her apartment at this time of night, and unannounced? She cautiously approached the door and took a quick look through the peephole.

What the hell?

"Are you crazy?" she asked quietly, opening the door. "Do you realize what time it I—" She stopped, taking in Will's red eyes and wrinkled shirt. "Hey... are you ok? Have you been *drinking*?"

That seemed to snap him out of his daze. "What? No! I... can I come in?"

"Of course. Remember to take off your shoes." Cameron stepped aside so he could enter, and he turned to face her as soon as he was inside. She was relieved that she didn't detect any alcohol on his breath. That was something she couldn't handle. She was barely handling herself.

"Did I wake you up?" He asked, bending to untie his sneakers, then slide them off of his feet.

Cameron raised an eyebrow. "You would know the answer to that if you had called first."

He gave her a sheepish grin before he turned to walked into the kitchen. She followed him, wondering what was going on. Things had been a little awkward between them since she made the misguided decision to sneak that kiss *near* his mouth, but he was acting downright weird.

"Will." She grabbed his hand, tugging on it until he turned to face her. "What's going on with you?"

He pulled his hand away, rubbing the back of his neck. "Are you gonna bug the shit out of me about it?"

So there *was* something wrong. Cameron was willing to ignore the fact that he was being rude after knocking on her door at 2am, because she saw something in his face that she never had before. Vulnerability. Something had him feeling raw and exposed, and he had decided to come *here*. To her.

What the hell does that *mean?*

"Not if you don't want me to. You hungry?"

Will tipped his head to the side, as if he were surprised that she had dropped it. Cameron knew better than to push. She hated it when people, with the exception of her therapist, did that to her. Hammering away at a weak spot until a person told you what you wanted to know, just to get you to shut up. Will never did that to her, and she wasn't about to do it to him.

When he nodded, she opened her refrigerator, pulling out the boxes of pizza she and Jai had ordered after the mishap with the spaghetti sauce. "I don't have any beer, but you can eat all the cold pizza you can hold."

"Why do you have so much?" he asked, sitting down at the counter.

"Jai is here."

He cringed. "How is she doing?"

"Pretty well, considering. She denied my offer to ask you to kick Derek's ass."

"He's so pitiful these days he probably wouldn't even notice it."

Cameron tried to hand Will a plate, but he waved it off, insisting that he would just eat from the box.

"You don't want to heat it up? I know I offered it cold, but ugh."

"I like it cold," he said, shrugging. "Let me eat how I want to."

He picked up the box and headed into the living room, settling comfortably onto her couch.

"Who told you it was ok to eat in my living room?" she asked, standing in front of him with her hands on her hips. Heat rushed to her face as his eyes swept down her body. Under his gaze she felt naked, but she wasn't uncomfortable. She felt *sexy*, standing in front of him with no panties or bra, only the yoga shorts and tank top she had

158

chosen after her shower clinging to her body. Barely containing a grin, she snapped her fingers in front of his face. "Hey, I asked you a question!"

"Can I eat in your living room, please?" He picked up another slice of pizza from the box, and proceeded to shove half of it into his mouth without waiting for a response.

Cameron rolled her eyes. "Whatever."

Will grabbed her hand, pulling her down beside him on the couch. "You want a bite?"

"No thanks," she responded, batting away the slice he was angling toward her face. "I'm not hungry." She reached over him for the remote, turning the TV to the comedy channel.

Cameron kept her focus on the TV while Will ate in silence. Nearly half an hour had passed before he finally said anything.

"Someone died, in the ambulance. A little girl."

She turned to him, but he wasn't looking at her. He kept his eyes trained on the TV as he spoke. "Fell off the jungle gym at school, landed at bad angle, right on her neck." He looked at Cameron and she nodded, urging him to go on. "She was barely breathing when we got there, but we had to try, you know? We tried *everything*."

Not knowing what to say, Cameron reached over and grabbed his hand.

"She looked *just like* Kelly. That little girl was only ten years old, the same age Kelly was when she got hit. But she was just... gone, before we could even pull out of the parking lot."

"Was that the first time you had someone die?"

He shook his head. "Nah. I've been doing this for nine years. She wasn't even the first child. It's not something you ever get used to, but you kinda become... I don't know, numb. But seeing a kid who looked like mine... it just kinda fucked me up today."

"I'm sorry that happened. Do you need a hug?"

"What? No, I don't need a hug."

"Wait, I phrased that wrong. I should have said 'I'm gonna give you a hug, ok?'"

"Could you stop?" Will asked, laughing as he halfheartedly tried to push Cameron away as she wrapped her arms around his neck, pulling herself closer until she was right against him. She suppressed a gasp when he hooked an arm under her legs, crossing them over his lap.

"What are you doing?"

He ran a hand over the bare skin of her leg, stopping when he reached the hem of her shorts. "What? I thought this is what you were trying to do."

"Yeah right." Cameron tried to swing her legs away, but Will maintained a gentle grip on her thigh.

"Leave 'em."

Their eyes met for a moment, but Cameron looked away, glancing down at his hand before her eyes found his again. Something had occurred to her.

"Who takes care of you, Will?"

He lifted an eyebrow. "Meaning?"

"You know, who do you talk to, who brings soup when you feel bad, that kind of thing?"

"I don't know. Derek and my brother I guess. And you."

"Me? Will, you don't talk to me. You *listen* to me, but you don't talk. Our friendship is super one-sided, actually. Why do you even hang out with me?"

Will shrugged. "What's with these questions?"

"I'm curious. I mean, I'm pretty boring, I'm a loner, and I'm super needy, always talking. I wasn't like that before the accident, but now? God, I'm like... a man's worst nightmare I think."

"I wouldn't say all of that," Will replied, laughing. "Maybe I like listening to you talk. I'm boring too, and prefer to not be in big crowds. And the neediness? Cameron you've been needy since I met you, the night of your accident."

"Now see, that's not funny," she said, smacking him in the chest.

"Yes it is. But seriously, you wanna know why I like hanging out with you?"

Cameron nodded.

"Cause *you* open your door at 2am, and don't ask a bunch of questions I don't wanna answer. And it helps that you're fine as hell, even with this thing on your head," he said, tugging at the satin scarf she had tied around her head to keep her hair protected as she slept. Before she could stop him, he had pulled it off, dropping it on the floor behind the couch.

"Do you have any idea how long it takes to tie that thing perfectly? Why would you do that?" She scolded.

He grinned. "Sorry."

"You're not."

"I'm not."

Cameron shrieked, trying to move away when he brought his hand up, running his fingers into her hair. "Will, what are you doing?"

"If you be still you'll find out."

Is he about to... Yes, he is!

His fingers were underneath her chin now, tilting her head back so that he could connect his lips with hers. Cameron squirmed, heat rushing to the space between her thighs as he gently gripped her backside before he—

"Cam!"

Jai's loud whisper from the hall instantly killed the heat. Cameron pushed Will away, trying to look innocent as her sister rounded the corner into the living room.

"Oh, it's just Will. Cam, you scared the shit out of me! I heard you scream and thought someone was in here attacking you!"

Cameron elbowed Will in the side as he chuckled. "I'm fine, Will was just playing around. But he's going home now."

"I am?"

"You are."

Chapter Twelve
— & —
Jai
Tuesday, March 24th

Shit.

Jai grimaced, struggling to maintain her grip on the pen as she scratched out yet another error on the inventory form. This wasn't one of her usual responsibilities, but the pain in her wrist had rendered her useless in the kitchen. Besides, being in Honeybee's cool, quiet pantry gave her an excuse not to talk to anyone. The last thing she wanted to do was field a bunch of questions about why she'd been moping for nearly a week. It wouldn't take long for everyone to realize that Derek wasn't popping up at the restaurant like he used to. After that, the gossip and sympathetic looks would start, getting more and more annoying until someone, probably one of the waitresses, would finally work up the nerve to just *ask* what happened.

At least, that's what happened after Elliot.

What kind of loser gets their heart broken three times in a year?

"This girl," she said aloud, gesturing at herself with her thumbs. She heard a sound behind her, and turned as heartbreaker #2 opened the pantry door. Jai cut her eyes away from him, back to the clipboard.

"Damn, we're not even speaking now?" Brian casually strode over to where Jai stood with her back to him. She felt him trying to look over her shoulder and pulled away, glancing back at him with a scowl.

"Did you need something?"

"No. I'm just worried about you," he said, following as she rounded one of the shelves. "And, I miss how things were between us before." Jai batted his hand away as he fingered the locs resting on her shoulder. She was angry, but not so much that she didn't still feel a pang in her chest at the reminder of their former friendship.

"Come *on*, Jai." She protested as he pulled the clipboard from her hands, tossing it onto the counter.

Jai hated herself for actually *enjoying* the embrace that he pulled her into. She even inhaled, breathing in the remnant aromas that the dinner service had left behind in his coat. She held that breath until he released her, taking a step back to give her some space.

"That wasn't so bad, was it?" he asked, using a finger to tip up her chin.

She shook her head. "I guess not."

Still, she moved away from his touch. All of his touchiness is what had gotten her in trouble in the first place. Now, she knew from experience that with Brian, she couldn't discern the difference between harmless flirting and foreplay. She wasn't about to fall back into that trap.

Apparently, Brian caught the hint, because he dropped his hands to his sides. "Listen... Jai, I'm sorry about everything that's happened. I haven't been the best friend I claimed to be. Can we put all of this crap behind us? Start fresh?"

Jai considered it as she turned to retrieve her forms. When she faced him again, she clutched the clipboard across her chest, searching his eyes for sincerity.

"Brian... I... Yeah." She nodded. "Yeah, we can start over. But only because I could really, really use a friend right now."

"What's going on? Did Derek do something to you?" Brian's fists were clenched as he sprang up from his relaxed position against the shelf.

"No!" Jai pressed a hand against Brian's chest to calm him down. "At least... not like that. He got his ex pregnant *after* he and I started dating."

The tension in his jaw relaxed, but the anger didn't leave his eyes. "He cheated on you?"

Jai squinted. "Well, technically no. It happened *after* I may have implied that we weren't really an item. I'm not even really mad that he slept with her, I'm just... hurt. I wish that he had pushed it a little harder. Maybe waited a little longer. Knowing that he slept with her makes me feel like he just gave up on us." She stopped, swallowing hard against the lump that was building in her throat.

"I'm so sorry, Jai." This time, when he embraced her, Jai crumpled into his arms, letting out the tears she'd been holding on to all day. She was grateful that he didn't say anything for a while, just let her cry against him. After a several long minutes, Jai lifted her head. Her eyes met Brian's and for a moment, she couldn't read his expression. But then his lips were on hers, so she closed her eyes, relaxing her body into his.

It was... *sweet*. She didn't feel tingly or hot or dizzy like when Derek kissed her. There wasn't even a sprinkle, let alone a *spark*. They pulled away at the same time, staring at each other for a moment until Jai broke into giggles. After a few seconds, Brian did the same, and they laughed until tears were rolling down their cheeks.

"That was so...."

"Awkward?" Brian finished, wiping his face with the backs of his hands.

Jai wrinkled her nose. "Extremely. All of this drama... and then *nothing*."

"Do you think Leslie will take me back?"

"Uhh..."

Brian grimaced. "Yeah, I didn't think so either."

"No, you should try." She put down the clipboard that had been crushed between them during their failed kiss. "I mean... when you guys kiss, it's not like what just happened with us, is it?"

"Not at all."

"Good. Then like I said, you should try. I'm sorry that I got all... Jai on you, and messed it up."

"Are you kidding? Jai, I've been in love with you on and off for probably six of the ten years we've known each other. Why do you think I hated Elliot?"

"Because he was an asshole."

Brian cocked his head to the side. "True. But I think I would have hated him anyway, just like I hated Derek. He had something I wanted, so I reacted like a little kid. Picking fights and shit. I always thought there might be something there between us, you were just the one with the um... *balls* to make a move on it."

Jai blinked, taking in what he said. "Wow. Brian, once everything kinda blew up... I thought that you were just leading me on because you could. I thought I was *crazy*. Like all of the flirting, the innuendo, I thought it was just playful for you, but I was taking it seriously."

"Well now you know. I was always flirting with you because I couldn't help it. I liked you. I still do."

Balancing on her elbows, Jai leaned forward onto the counter. "But maybe that's just the effect of the close proximity, you know? We've been super close for a *decade*, and never even kissed until now."

"What about when you kissed me at your apartment?"

"You mean when you dumped my ass on the floor," Jai laughed. "I'm not counting that, because you were an unwilling participant. I'm just saying, I think that maybe the attraction of the unknown made of friendly feelings seem like something they weren't."

Brian leaned onto the table across from her. "Maybe so. Whatever it was… I think the possibility has passed." He extended his hand to her. "Friends again?"

"What?" Jai sucked her teeth. "Brian, if you don't get your ass around the table and give me a hug! What am I supposed to do with a handshake, man?"

After they hugged, Jai smiled. It felt good, better than she had expected, to have her friend back after the last few strained months. She reached for her pen again, to finally finish taking inventory, but she just couldn't maintain her grip. Frustrated, she made another attempt, but as her hand closed around the pen, she felt a snap. She gasped as white heat shot through her fingers and up her arm.

"Jai! Jai, what's going on? What happened?" Jai could hear Brian talking to her, but couldn't make herself respond. She couldn't make herself do anything, she could only register the scorching pain radiating from her wrist. Then, everything went black.

— & —
Derek
Wednesday, March 25th

"Is this gonna be over soon?"

Cameron let out an annoyed sigh as Derek put his hands on her shoulders, stopping her calf raises. She had been like this for the entire length of the session, sucking her teeth, rolling her eyes, and cursing him out under her breath. If her intent was to make their last session as miserable as possible, she was hitting her target.

Derek was actually a little surprised that she wasn't giving him the blatant attitude she had in their early sessions after their accident.

But, the two of them had formed a friendship of their own, and Derek suspected that Cameron was having a hard time keeping up her mean act. That suspicion was confirmed halfway through the session, when she looked him right in the eyes, and said "Jai is here."

Here?

Heart racing, his first instinct was to look behind him, toward the open gym door. He then glanced around the room, and not spotting her, turned back to Cameron. "Here where?"

"In the hospital."

Derek's stomach roiled and his palms immediately went clammy as he dropped down onto one of the weight benches behind them. "In the hospital?" He repeated, choking the question past the sudden dryness in his throat. "Why is she in—?"

"Her wrist," Cameron interrupted, "A tendon ruptured in her wrist while she was at Honeybee last night. She had surgery on this morning."

"What floor?"

His nostrils flared when Cameron didn't answer, bending instead to tie her shoelace. "What if she doesn't want to see you?" she asked when she stood.

"I wanna see *her*."

"So?" she challenged, crossing her arms as she stepped forward. "You broke her heart. Why should I give a shit what you want?"

"You realize I'm a contractor for the hospital, right? I can find out what room she's in."

"Ah, but you can't get in. Restricted visitors list."

Shit.

Derek rubbed the back of his neck, pushing out a heavy breath. "Cameron…."

"Derek…."

"*Please.*"

Cameron's expression was still grim when she stepped forward. "She made me promise not to tell you when she found out today was my last session. But, she didn't say that I couldn't tell you she was being discharged this afternoon, and she's staying at her apartment."

Derek let out a sigh of relief. "Do you think she'll see me?"

"Depends on what you have to say for yourself." She sat down beside him on the bench. "I'm going to tell you something that I probably shouldn't... but I want to see my sister happy, so I'm gonna tell you anyway."

"Thank you."

Cameron smirked. "Don't thank me yet. Derek, Jai isn't really tripping about you sleeping with that girl. She knows she messed up when she did that 'you're not my man, can't tell me what to do' crap. She *owns* that. But, the fact that you *did* sleep with her... to Jai, it meant that she wasn't that important to you. If you could just immediately run to sleep with someone else, she feels like she must not have mattered very much to you then. But you mattered a *lot* to her. Do you see?"

"I do, but she has it messed up. Jai has pretty much always been important to me. That's why I got so pissed off and ended up fucking everything up." Derek scratched his head. "That's something I *can't* fix."

"What's with men these days? Just making a habit of unprotected sex with exes, it's gross," she said, curling her lip.

"I used protection with Jessica."

Cameron lifted an eyebrow. "And she got pregnant? Whose protection did you use?"

"My own. I got it out of my wallet. Why?"

"People are sneaky these days, you have to ask. If it were me? I'd be at her next appointment, making sure everything is legit. I don't think you little baby mama can be trusted."

— & —
Wednesday Afternoon

"What the hell do you mean no?"

"Derek...did I stutter?"

Glaring at Jessica from across her kitchen counter, Derek pulled open the bag he had brought inside with him. "Fine. You say I can't go to an appointment with you, I want you take another pregnancy test." He slapped one down, sliding it across the smooth granite surface.

"What?" She gripped the edge of the counter, staring down at the pink and white box for a moment before looking up. "I'm not doing this."

"Jessica, if I have to drag you into that bathroom myself, you're taking the damn test."

"You wouldn't dare touch me. Don't want to hurt the baby." She patted her stomach with a smirk. In the week that had passed since she first broke the news, she showing now. Just barely, but that hadn't stopped her from adopting the 'pregnant woman's' waddle. "I'm going to lie down. Show yourself out, *daddy*."

Derek fought back nausea as he watched her waddle out of the room with her hand resting on her belly. He had to get out of there, and figure out how he could possibly make things right with Jai. As he approached the front door, his eyes fell on the side table. Jessica's purse was turned on its side, most of the contents scattered on the table. His heart raced as he reached for the bright white appointment card for Jessica's OB-GYN, the handwritten message on the side reminding her to come in for her fourteen week appointment.

"Fourteen?" He asked himself out loud. That couldn't be right. He quickly calculated the length of time since when he had slept with Jessica. She would have to be almost twenty weeks right now. He looked at the card again, searching for the date. Maybe it was an old appointment card. He smiled, bigger than he had in days when found it. This card was definitely for Jessica's fourteen week appointment.

Next week.

— & —
Cameron
Wednesday Night

Cameron groaned as she pulled her shopping cart to an abrupt stop to avoid hitting the speeding cart being pushed around the corner.

I knew I should have just ordered Chinese.

Seven o'clock at night in the middle of the week definitely wasn't an ideal time to be at the grocery store, and yet it seemed like *everyone* was there, and they were all in a rush. Cameron was starting to get a headache. There were too many people, too much traffic, and too much hassle. All she wanted was the ingredients to make a decent salad, and maybe one of those pre-cooked chickens. Jai would disapprove, but Cameron was fending for herself tonight. Jai had painkillers and a smoothie for dinner, passing out soon after. So, after threatening to castrate him if he touched her sister, Cameron had left Jai in Rashad's care, while Brian handled the restaurant, and *she* went home to get some rest in own bed.

The steady routine helped a lot. Generally speaking, as long as things were kept in passable order, the craving for a drink remained at bay. Cameron's therapist had just presented her with her three-month sobriety token, and she reached into the pocket of her jacket to finger the cold metal ridges along the side.

It's ok. You're ok.

"Cameron?"

For a moment, her knees were weak. She released her coin so that she could use both hands to grip the handle of the cart for support.

"Kyle. Uh... hi."

Cameron sagged against the cart, closing her eyes to stop the sensation that the room was spinning. She needed a second, just a little break from—

"Found it! Kyle, I got the..." The woman's voice trailed off, and Cameron assumed that she had been spotted by the other member of Kyle's new little family.

Her stomach lurched, and she clamped her eyes shut even harder.

Please, just disappear.

"Cameron? Are you ok?" This was a nightmare. It had to be. She opened her eyes and glanced at Angie's left hand, and felt light-headed. She couldn't breathe. *Married?* He had married her?

Stop spazzing, Cameron. You're ok. It's just Kyle. And Angie and her baby bump. But you're ok.

"Yes, I'm fine! I'm ok. Just... surprised to run into you guys," she said, plastering on a smile.

They both returned her smile, but exchanged looks before turning back to Cameron.

They think I'm crazy.

Maybe she was. She had spent a disgusting amount of time covering the subject of Kyle in therapy, and she thought she was over it. Well, not *over* it, but far enough past it that just seeing him wouldn't induce panic. It had been nearly four months since she'd seen either of them, but the hurt came flooding back like it was brand new. She couldn't do this. She had to get away, now.

Cameron's eyes darted over to Angie. She was disappointed that instead of looking ragged and worn down, like she'd hoped, Angie had maintained her angelic prettiness, even when she was hugely pregnant. They made eye contact for a few seconds before Angie dropped her eyes. "I'm just gonna go and wait for you, ok Kyle?" Angie couldn't get away fast enough, whipping the cart back the way they had come.

When they were alone, Cameron took the time to study Kyle. She had done such an effective job of trying to forget him that his face had become fuzzy in her memories. He was back in high-definition now, still handsome as ever.

"So," he said, taking a step closer. "How have you been?"

Miserable.

"I've been ok. I'm fine. You?"

"About the same."

Cameron's eyes traveled down to the wedding band on his left ring finger. "I see you got married. Well, remarried, I guess."

"Yeah. It was important to Angie."

"But not to you?" He blinked, realizing his gaffe.

"No, it's important to me too. We uh… we worked it out."

Nausea swept through her as she tried to smile. "That's good. I'm… happy for you. Congratulations."

He swept a hand over his head, massaging the base of his neck. "Thanks. What about you? Are you seeing anyone?"

"No. I'm still just… enjoying the single life again I guess."

Why are you asking me this? Why am I still talking to you?

His expression softened into something Cameron couldn't stand. Sympathy. Ugh. "I'm sure someone will be along to snag you soon. You're really an incredible woman Cameron."

"Not enough to keep you from someone else though. So maybe incredible is a stretch. But I appreciate that you're trying to make me feel better about being alone. Really," she lied. Did he honestly think that those words out of *his* mouth would make her feel good? Didn't they all say that? "You're so awesome, I was just too stupid to see it." It was bullshit.

"My infidelity had nothing to do with you. If you don't believe anything else I say, believe that. The affair was *my* mistake, Cameron. I'm just trying to make the best out of this."

Kyle took another step forward and grabbed her hand. "Cameron, can you look at me? I need you to know I'm sorry. I never, *ever* intended to hurt you."

"I know, Kyle." Her voice broke as she pulled her hand away

from his. She put it back in her pocket, fingering her three month coin as if it held some invisible strength. "But you did, and I'm still dealing with that, so if you're looking for forgiveness... I can't give you that right now." She had tried, in therapy, but she still couldn't make herself utter those words. She wasn't even angry anymore, but the pain and the sense of betrayal remained.

His shoulders slumped. "I understand."

"Yeah. You should get back to your wife." She tried not to sound bitter. She was supposed to be *past* bitter. Cameron didn't want to become that girl.

"Probably so. We just ran in for some kind of fancy cheese she was talking about." He glanced into her cart. "Look like you're grabbing dinner too. The only thing you're missing is your bottle of wine."

Cameron's heart thumped and she released her hold on the token. "You know what? You're right." She gave him a tight smile, then turned to walk away.

To get her bottle of wine.

— & —
Will
Late Wednesday Night

Will woke up with a jolt. At first, he thought the loud banging was coming from the TV, which playing the same bass-filled tune over and over as the DVD's menu screen repeated it's opening sequence. Grabbing the remote, he switched it off. He hadn't been home very long.

After his shift, he had gone home and showered, then ordered way more Chinese food than anyone needed in one night. He ate, then settled on his couch to watch a movie. Anything to keep his mind off of Cameron and her faint scent of citrus and vanilla. And those long, perfect legs. And those lush, juicy lips that he had almost gotten to taste. He made a mental note to foul Derek *hard* next time they were on the basketball court. It was his damn fault that Jai had been there. Who knows what would have happened if she hadn't been there?

Maybe nothing. Or maybe that night would have set the precedent for him to fall asleep in front of the TV with his hands full of *Cameron*, instead of a remote.

Shit.

This was Cameron's fault too. That little sneaky corner-of-the-mouth kiss of hers had started something, and Will really, really wanted to finish it. His head shot up. There was the banging *again*. He realized then that it was coming from his front door. Groaning, he pulled himself up from the couch and went to answer it.

There she was. The object of his fantasies had appeared at his door, soaking wet from the rain that had started earlier in the night. She looked distressed, and one good look at her puffy, red eyes told him that it wasn't because she had gotten wet. She'd been crying.

Without a word, he pulled her inside, intending to take her into the bathroom to strip off her soaked clothes. The distinct clinking of glass stopped him in his tracks. He glanced down, noticing the grocery bag in her hand for the first time. He took it from her and looked inside, frowning at the bag's contents.

"Cameron, did you...?"

Will's shoulders sagged with relief when she shook her head. He put the bag on the counter, then pushed her through his bedroom into his bathroom, where he helped her out of her wet clothes. When she was down to her underwear, he averted his eyes, handing her a towel before he went into the laundry room to find something clean of Kelly's that she could wear. He dropped off a pair of shorts and a tee shirt at the door, then headed back into the kitchen.

Standing at the sink, he pulled a bottle of vodka and two bottles of wine from the bag Cameron had brought with her. What the hell was she thinking? Was she planning to drink *all* of this? He couldn't help feeling disappointed as he opened all three and poured them down the drain, then tossed the bottles in the trash. She had just gotten her three month token *yesterday*.

What the fuck happened?

When thirty minutes had passed without Cameron making an appearance, Will went to find her. He chuckled when he saw the lump in the middle of his bed, created by Cameron's body under the sheets. He didn't think twice about climbing in behind her, then turning her to face him.

Will felt an ache starting in his throat when he realized she was crying again. "Hey," he reached forward, cupping her face in his hand. "What happened?"

"Kyle."

Anger bubbled in his chest at the sound of that name. "What

did he do now?"

"Nothing. I just bumped into him at the store, with his wife and her *belly*."

"Wife?"

Cameron gave him a tight smile through her tears. "Yep. They got married. I didn't think I would care, but when I saw them, I just kinda lost it."

"Oh man, what did you do?"

"I didn't *do* anything. We talked for a few minutes and then went our separate ways."

Will brushed her hair back from her forehead, fingering the curls that had been revealed by the rain. "Do you feel better?"

"Not really," she sniffled. "Seeing him just brought it all back."

"So you thought you would get drunk and it would go away again."

Cameron brought her eyes up to meet his as she nodded. "Once I had it… it just didn't even seem all that appealing. It didn't feel worth it, because I knew it wouldn't make me feel any better. But I knew coming to you would."

"How did you know I would open the door?"

"Because I opened the door for you. And I know Kelly is with her mom during the week, so I figured you weren't busy."

"And what if I was?" He trailed his fingers along the side of her face, down to her neck. "What if I had company?"

"I would have been completely embarrassed, and I'm pretty sure I would have cracked open that vodka."

Will laughed as he continued to move his hand along her body, traveling over her shoulder, and stopping at her waist. He fingered the hem of her shirt, considering his next move before deciding to go for it, slipping his hand underneath to touch the bare skin at her side.

"Kyle said something that really bothered me."

"What's that?"

"Some crap about me being so awesome, it wasn't me, it was him. That kind of thing."

"Why do you say its crap?"

Cameron shrugged. "I mean… I get that he had the history with his ex, and that those feelings were still there. But if he thought so highly of me, why wouldn't he just break up with me instead of cheating? Or, just not cheat, you know?"

"People do dumb shit when they're in love. It's not always pretty, and it's not always black and white. I really, really hate to say anything in that motherfucker's defense, but Kyle still loving his ex doesn't mean that he didn't love you. He just ended up in a fucked up situation, and Angie being pregnant made his decision for him. I mean, from what you told me, it sounded like he had chosen you."

"He did," Cameron admitted. "But he and Angie looked happy, so I guess he ended up with his better option anyway."

"Will you stop that?"

"Stop what? It's the truth. He got his first choice back; I was just his rebound, obviously."

Will sighed, then propped himself up on his elbow. With the other hand, he turned her face toward his. "Cameron, you are smart, funny, successful, and sexy as hell. You're not anybody's second choice."

"Whatev—"

She let the word trail off when he moved closer to her, so close that their lips were almost touching. "What are you doing?"

Will answered by brushing his lips against hers.

So damn soft.

A low, sensual moan escaped Cameron's mouth as Will kissed her again, and that was all it took for his erection to spring to life, straining against the soft cotton of his boxers. She looped her arms around his neck, pulling him closer until he was on top of her, balancing his weight on his forearms. He found the hem of her shirt again and slipped a hand underneath, cupping her breast as he swirled her tongue with his.

"*Will,*" she gasped, gripping his head as he moved down to her neck, gently nipping her between kisses. "What are we doing?"

"Nothing yet." He took his mouth further south, kissing her hardened nipples through the flimsy fabric of the tee shirt before he broke away to pull it over her head. The shirt dropped from his hands as he sat back, staring down at Cameron's topless body. Then he had to touch her again. As he took turns tasting the dark brown peaks of her breasts, he gripped the waistband of her shorts, yanking them down her hips.

When his fingers found the moist heat between her legs, she arched her hips closer to him in response as he slid them inside of her. She wrapped an arm around his neck as he hungrily kissed her, rolling her hips frantically as he continued to stroke. The other hand she snaked between them, slipping into his boxers to grip the erection that was now impossibly hard.

"Will, *please?*" She moaned the breathless request into his shoulder, her legs shaking as he pushed his fingers as deep as they would go. Without waiting for a response, she impatiently began to tug his boxers down, freeing him from the restrictive fabric.

At this point, Will was aching to be inside of her, but he reluctantly separated himself from her to retrieve a condom from the bedside drawer. When he approached the bed again, she had wrapped herself in the sheet, clutching it to her body as she stared up at him.

"What's wrong?" he asked, pulling the sheet away just enough to crawl under with her before he pulled it tight around them. *Please don't tell me you're changing your mind.*

"Nothing." Will groaned as Cameron lowered her hand to his erection again, giving it a firm squeeze. "It's just... if we do this... what does that mean for us?"

Does she have to stroke my dick while we talk about this?

His fingers found her opening again and he pushed inside, eliciting a soft gasp from her. "I don't know. What do you want it to mean?"

"I... uh... shit, I don't know. I just wanna know that this wasn't your goal all along."

Will nearly laughed. "Cameron, I know you don't think I've been your friend for three months for just a *chance* to get inside of you, do you?" He gently caught one of her nipples between his teeth, putting on slight pressure before he sucked it into his mouth.

She threw her head back, moaning her pleasure before she found the composure to speak. "I mean... I don't *think* a guy that looks like you would have to work so hard for sex, but you never know."

"I don't. And remember, I didn't even like you at first. Your pussy may as well have been radioactive as far as I was concerned."

"I still can't stand you," Cameron whispered as he positioned himself on top of her, wrapping her legs around his. Will kissed her, gently pushing his tongue into her mouth to taste her again before he slowly entered her, taking his time so she could adjust to him.

Damn she feels good.

"Why you lyin', Cam? You know you like me."

175

"Uh-uh. I don't." She dug her nails into his back as she rolled her hips, meeting his thrusts with her own. She shifted, hooking her legs around his waist and he slid deeper. "Mmmmm. Maybe a little."

Will stroked faster. "Just a little?"

She didn't respond. Or maybe she did, but it was mixed in with her sexy little sighs and moans of pleasure. He struggled to take it easy with her instead of giving in to the overwhelming desire to shove himself into her as fast, hard, and far as he possibly could. And she was making it, and him, *so fucking hard*. Cameron was constantly moving, effortlessly keeping pace with his rhythm. And then there were the things she was whispering in his ear, nasty little encouragements and desperate requests for 'faster, harder' that soon had him forgetting his decision to take it easy. A few moments later, she was pulsing around him, hot and slick as he pushed inside her one last time before his own release.

Will rolled off of her, not wanting to crush her under his weight. When she snuggled close to him, resting her head against his chest, it felt strangely comfortable, the opposite of how he usually felt when women wanted to cuddle after sex. It was... nice. He liked it.

He liked *her*.

— & —
Jai
Thursday, March 26

"GET OUT!" Jai flung open the glass shower door, using her left hand to throw her bottle of body wash at Rashad's head. When she woke up that morning, she had carefully wrapped the cast on her wrist in plastic, sealing it with tape so that she could take a much needed hot shower after the events of the last two days. The last thing she had expected to see when she turned to let the shower spray was Rashad's shocked face, staring.

What the hell had Cameron been thinking, leaving him of all people to stay with her while she slept? Furious, Jai stepped out of the tiled shower and grabbed a towel, hastily wrapping it around herself before she stalked out of the bathroom to find Rashad. When she found him, sitting in the kitchen at the bar, she used her casted arm to keep her towel closed around her body while the left rained open slaps down on Rashad's head and face.

"Damnit, Jai! Would you stop?! I wasn't watching you, I was

peeking in make sure you were ok!"

She stopped hitting him, but pointed a sharp finger in his face. "Liar! You were standing there staring, with your mouth hanging open!"

"It's not *my* fault you look like that! I'm a man, Jai. I saw wet, naked ass. Hell yeah, I looked!"

"Ugh!" She hit him one last time before she turned to stalk away.

"Jai, wait a minute." Rashad jumped up from his seat, blocking her exit from the kitchen. "You know, since you're already naked under that towel, we cou—"

"Rashad, we've talked about this, ok? I'm really not in the mood for your games. Can you cut it out, please?"

He instantly sobered. "Jai, you know I don't mean any disrespect, right?"

"I know, but I'm still not feeling it right now, ok? Just chill."

Rashad grabbed her hand, pulling it up to his mouth for a kiss. "I'm sorry, ok? I can lay off on the flirting; I don't wanna make you uncomfortable. My girlfriend would probably kick my ass anyway."

"Girlfriend?!" Jai snatched her hand away. "You're in here watching me in the shower, but you have a girlfriend? Little boy, you gotta go home. No-no-no, I *refuse* to have another crazy ass girl running up on me, thinking I'm trying to take her man."

She made Rashad walk in front of her to the door, which she opened, then unceremoniously pushed him outside. She didn't even say goodbye, simply closed the door behind him. A few seconds later, he was knocking again. She rolled her eyes as she flung it open.

"Listen, nobody is playing with you. Take your little nasty ass right back— Oh! Derek."

Her heart slammed in her chest at the sight of his handsome face. His steel blue eyes seemed more striking than she remembered. His shoulders seemed broader than before, and Jai could swear he had a few more subtle brown freckles against his golden skin.

"Hey Beautiful... can we talk?"

"Uhh, yeah." She moved aside so that he could step in, and she closed the door behind him. She followed him into the living and sat down beside him the couch, keeping her towel clutched carefully around her body.

"I heard you had surgery," he said, pointing at her wrist. "You shouldn't hold it like that." He reached forward, gently shifting the position of her arm. "You'll get better blood flow like this."

"Thanks. It probably would have been worse, if I'd kept taking those stupid antibiotics. I'm glad you were there to take them from me, and tell me about them."

"Me too. You're still gonna need a physical therapist though, if you want to get back in the kitchen sooner after you heal."

"I have one."

Derek's jaw clenched. Jai knew he was probably a little hurt that she hadn't called him, but what was she supposed to say? *'Hey, I know I broke up with you, but I need you to take time out of your schedule to help me.'*

"I see. I should probably get to why I came by then, and get out of your way." He smiled at her, but it didn't reach his eyes. "I just wanted to tell you that I found out some good news. It's about Jessica."

"She's not really pregnant?"

Please let it be that, please let it be that!

"No, she's definitely pregnant." *Shit.* "But it's definitely not mine."

Jai's heart leapt to her throat. Using her left hand, she grabbed Derek's shoulder. "Are you serious? How do you know?"

"She's not even fourteen weeks pregnant yet! And I know I wasn't anywhere near her then. She would have to be a lot further along for it to be mine."

"What?! She told you this?"

Derek shook his head. "Hell no. She would have denied it till the end, but I found her appointment card, with the information on it. When I showed her that, she couldn't even talk her way out of it. She just started crying and told me everything."

Jai couldn't stop a broad smile from spreading across her face. "That's great for you! I wonder what she thought was going to happen when she was a whole month late having the baby?"

"I don't know, and I don't care. I'm just hoping it can be great for *us*." He cupped her face in his hands. "Jai... tell me what I have to do to get us past this?"

"Well now that you don't have a *baby* on the way, I just want you to be invested, Derek. It seemed like it was way too easy for you to run to another woman."

"I am, Jai. I love you, girl, you know what." Jai shivered as Derek's hand drifted down to skim the top of her towel. "I'm not going anywhere. You're stuck with me now." Her nipples immediately hardened, responding to his touch. She knew she had missed Derek, but she didn't realize how much her *body* missed him until he leaned forward, capturing her lips in a kiss.

"I love you too," she whispered when they finally separated. "Now can you do me a favor?"

"Anything, baby."

"My arm is killing me; please bring me my painkillers from the kitchen, and a glass of water?"

He planted a kiss on her forehead as he stood. "Of course, baby."

Less than a minute later, he was walking back in. Jai laughed as he froze in the doorway, nearly dropping the things in his hands.

"What are you doing, Derek?"

"I… uh…" His eyes traveled to the towel on the floor, then back up to Jai, who was wearing nothing but her cast and a smile.

"Mmm hmm. Can you hurry up and bring me those pills?"

He did, keeping his eyes focused on her body. Jai was pleased to see the erection straining against the front of his pants as he watched her. She quickly downed the pills, took a drink, then sat the glass down on the table as she stood. She grabbed his hand, then raised herself up on her toes to kiss him.

"Now… come show me how much you missed me."

— & —
Jai
Friday, April 24th

Jai looked up, smiling as Brian walked through the door. Her happy expression slipped when she noticed the somber look on his face.

"Brian… what's wrong?"

"Uh… I found a position at another restaurant."

Jai's eyes widened. "A new position? Why do you need another job? Are you not making enough? We can talk about salary if—"

"Jai. If you would let me talk…"

179

"Oh. Sorry."

Brian sat down, clasping his hands in front of him on the desk. "You remember a few weeks ago, when I told you that Leslie finally took me back?"

"Of course."

"Well... one of her conditions was that she didn't want me working with you anymore."

"Oh... well, I think that if I were her, I wouldn't be too happy about you working with me either." Jai sat back in her chair, crossing her arms.

"Yeah. I thought that was fair, after everything that happened, so I agreed to it. She was fine with me holding Honeybee down for you while you recovered from your surgery, but now that you're back... it's time for me to move on."

Jai gave Brian a sad smile. She completely understood his desire to make things work with Leslie, and she supported that. Honestly, she was glad to see that he was willing to put forth such an effort for her. Still, it hurt a little that they would no longer be working together, after being so close for more than a decade.

"Do what you have to do, B. I'll give you a glowing reference."

"Duh, Jai," he said laughing. "And I'm sorry for not telling you sooner, I just didn't want you thinking about that while you were already so stressed with everything else. I'll be here at least another month and I've already started looking for my replacement."

"So you thought of everything already?"

"Hey, I try."

Jai smiled, holding out her arms for a hug. When they separated, she stepped back, admiring Brian's dark blue suit. "So is Leslie ok with today?"

"Ok with it? She's thrilled."

Relieved, Jai turned back to the full length mirror, smoothing her hands over the tulle skirt of her sunny yellow dress.

"You look beautiful, Jai." Cameron stepped back in, holding two bouquets of white roses in her hands. She handed one to Jai, keeping the other for herself as the reach up, tucking a stray loc back into Jai's intricate bun. "Are you ready?"

Jai nodded, looking between Brian and Cameron.

"Definitely."

180

— & —
Cameron

"I can't believe those fools got married." Will approached Cameron from behind, pushing a champagne glass into her hand. "Ginger ale," he said, in response to the scowl she gave him *and* the drink.

"Oh." She smiled. "Thank you."

They turned, watching as Derek and Jai shared their first dance as husband and wife, in the middle of Honeybee's dining room floor. "They look so happy," Cameron whispered up to Will, even as she continued watching the couple. "It's sweet."

"It's crazy. They've only known each for what, seven months now?"

Cameron nodded. "Yep. They met a few months after my accident, and they've liked each since that first day I think. He proposed to her the day after they got back together because he needed to prove he was committed. That's the trouble with love. You never know when you'll lose it, when you'll find it, or what you'll have to do to keep it. But they really, really love each other. For them... it's not crazy at all. "

"For them? So you're saying it would be crazy for you."

"Heck yeah. I think I would run away screaming if somebody pulled out a ring to give me after such a short time."

Will gently grabbed her shoulder, pulling her around to face him. "Give me your hand."

"What?"

"I said give me your hand."

She snatched away from him, hiding her hands behind her back. "Hell no, Will! What's your problem?!"

"Damn, simmer down." Cameron stiffened as he took her hand, slipping something into her palm. As soon as her fingers closed around it, she knew what it was.

"How do you always manage to get these before me?" she asked, smiling down at the four-month sober token in her hand.

"Cause I got it like that."

"Mmhm. Thank you baby. I'm just glad it's this, and not a ring." She relaxed into his body, allowing him place a soft, sweet kiss on her lips.

He glanced around, making sure no one was looking before he palmed her backside. "I like you, but not *that* much."

"Good. I don't like you that much either."

"Cameron," Rashad called out as he approached. "Jai is ready for pictures."

She turned to follow him, but Will caught her hand and squeezed.

"Hey. I love you..."

Cameron smiled, giving him a squeeze back. "I love you too."

— *the end* —

Thank you for reading! If you enjoyed this book, please consider leaving me a review.
You can visit with me at www.beingmrsjones.com or
https://www.facebook.com/Christinacjones
I'm also on twitter, at @beingmrsjones

Made in the USA
Middletown, DE
31 July 2017